"You are unusual,"  you believe me?"

She took another hasty sip. The rich, heady wine flowed down her throat and wrapped around her chest like a winter quilt.

She let her gaze wander over to the blue spruce expertly decorated with glass baubles and ribbon bows in the corner. Jace Ryan might be a lot more man than she felt capable of handling. But where was the harm in enjoying his company. At least for as long as it took to clean her coat.

"How exactly am I unusual?" she asked, knowing it wasn't true, but happy to have him try to persuade her.

He placed his beer bottle on the coffee table and stood up. Lifting her hand from her lap, he wrapped his long fingers around it and gave a soft tug to pull her off the sofa. "Stand up, so we can examine the evidence."

She did as she was told, the appreciative gleam as his gaze roamed over her, shocking her into silence.

"Your eyes are a really unusual colour. I noticed that as soon as you jumped into my car. Even though you were ruining the upholstery and calling me a jerk."

"I only called you a jerk because you were being a jerk," she pointed out in her defence.

He placed his hands on her hips. "Stop ruining the mood."

"What mood?" she asked, standing so close to him now she could see the gold flecks in his irises.

The buckle on his belt brushed against her tummy and the little shivers became shock waves, shuddering down to the place between her thighs.

"The mood I'm trying to create" he said, a lock of dark hair flopping over his brow. "So I can kiss you."

HEIDI RICE was born and bred—and still lives—in London, England. She has two boys who love to bicker, a wonderful husband who, luckily for everyone, has loads of patience, and a supportive and ever-growing British/French/Irish/American family. As much as Heidi adores "the Big Smoke," she also loves America, and every two years or so she and her best friend leave hubby and kids behind and *Thelma and Louise* it across the States for a couple of weeks (although they always leave out the driving-off-a-cliff bit). She's been a film buff since her early teens and a romance junkie for almost as long. She indulged her first love by being a film reviewer for ten years. Then two years ago, she decided to spice up her life by writing romance. Discovering the fantastic sisterhood of romance writers (both published and unpublished) in Britain and America made it a wild and wonderful journey to her first Harlequin novel, and she's looking forward to many more to come.

Books by Heidi Rice

Harlequin Presents® Extra

124—UNFINISHED BUSINESS WITH THE DUKE
147—SURF, SEA AND A SEXY STRANGER

Other titles by this author available in eBook

ON THE FIRST NIGHT
OF CHRISTMAS...
HEIDI RICE

~ 'Tis the Season to be Tempted ~

TORONTO NEW YORK LONDON
AMSTERDAM PARIS SYDNEY HAMBURG
STOCKHOLM ATHENS TOKYO MILAN MADRID
PRAGUE WARSAW BUDAPEST AUCKLAND

Recycling programs
for this product may
not exist in your area.

ISBN-13: 978-0-373-52843-1

ON THE FIRST NIGHT OF CHRISTMAS...

First North American Publication 2011

Copyright © 2011 by Heidi Rice

ON THE FIRST NIGHT
OF CHRISTMAS...

To my Mum and Dad,
for so many wonderful Christmas memories

CHAPTER ONE

IF ONLY my love life were as perfect as Selfridges at Christmas.

Cassie Fitzgerald let out a wistful sigh as she gazed at the explosion of festive bling in the iconic London store's window display. The Sugar Plum Fairy sparkled flirtatiously on the shoulder of a hunky mannequin dressed in a dinner suit, silver snowflake lights making her tiny wings twinkle. Cassie's heart lifted. Selfridges' Christmas window dressing never let you down. It always captured the hope and expectation of the season of goodwill so beautifully. And okay, maybe her love life wasn't perfect—in fact, it was non-existent—but that was still a big improvement on last year.

A frown creased Cassie's brow as she recalled the Christmas wish she'd made the year before while standing in front of Selfridges—involving Lance, her boyfriend of three years, and a proposal of marriage.

She wrinkled her nose in disgust, the frozen air making it tingle, as her mind conjured up the image of Lance and Tracy McGellan getting up close and pornographic on the sofa in Cassie's flat a month after Valentine's Day. A month after Cassie had accepted that wished-for proposal.

Colour hit her cheeks as she remembered her shock and disbelief, swiftly followed by the shame of her own idiocy.

What on earth had possessed her to agree to marry a deadbeat like Lance?

As Christmas wishes went, it was one of her worst. Right up there with wishing for a pair of inline skates when she was eight—which had resulted in a broken wrist and four hours in Accident and Emergency on Christmas Day. Marriage to Lance would have been worse, but in her typically romantic fashion she'd overlooked all his shortcomings, determined to convince herself that he was The One.

Cassie hunched her shoulders against the brisk winter wind. From now on she was going to stop looking at life through rose-tinted glasses...because all it did was blind her to reality. And she wasn't making a Christmas wish this year, because it might come true.

It would be a shame not to have anyone to wake up with this Christmas morning—and she'd been in a funk about it for days. She adored bounding out of bed, brewing a pot of spiced apple tea and then savouring the presents artfully arranged under the tree. Having to do all that alone wasn't quite the same.

But as her best friend Nessa had pointed out, Cassie was better off doing it alone than with Lance the Loser. Cassie huddled in her coat. Absorbing the bright sparkle of Sugar Plum and her beau, she let the thought of her lucky escape from Lance strengthen her resolve.

'What you need is a candy man—to give your girly bits a wake-up call. Then you wouldn't need another deadbeat boyfriend.'

Cassie's lips edged up as she recalled Nessa's use-him-then-lose-him advice when they'd chatted on the phone that morning. Sometimes she really wished she could be as pragmatic about sex as Nessa. If she could just take sex a little less seriously, maybe she could have some fun without getting tangled up with creeps like Lance.

Bidding goodbye to Sugar Plum, Cassie jostled her way to Bond Street tube. Frantic shoppers herded in and out of the shops along Oxford Street on a mission to buy all those essential last-minute items that would make their Christmas complete. Stopping at the kerb as the traffic barrelled past on one of the cross streets, Cassie squeezed her eyes shut and fantasised about her candy man. Hot, hunky and devoted to making her feel fabulous, he would be magically gone by the New Year—so she'd never have to spend time picking his socks up off the bathroom floor, or washing the dirty dishes he left piled in the sink, or persuading herself she was in love with him.

Her erogenous zones zinged pleasantly for the first time in months.

She opened her eyes as the roar of a car engine interrupted the warm, fuzzy glow. Then shrieked as a wall of freezing water slammed into her. The elderly gentleman next to her muttered, 'Damn inconsiderate,' as a puddle the size of the Atlantic sluiced back into the gutter, and a sleek black car sped past.

Cassie gasped. The warm, fuzzy glow replaced by ice-cold shock. 'What the…!'

The driver hadn't even stopped. What a prize jerk.

Flinging her bag over her shoulder, she turned to glare at the vehicle, which had braked at the crossing ten feet away. Her fingers curled into tight fists at her sides.

Normally, she would have let the matter pass. Normally, she would have chalked the drenching up to bad luck and assumed the driver hadn't meant to splash her. But as she stood there, the other shoppers edging past her and gawping at the huge wet patch on her favourite coat as if she had a contagious disease, she felt something new and liberating surging up her torso.

Whether he'd meant to do it or not, she was soaked. And she wasn't going to just stand by and take whatever life had to throw at her any more.

Dodging through the crowd, she drew level and rapped on the passenger window. 'Hey, Ebenezer.'

The tinted glass slid down with an electric hum. She blinked, the zing tingling back to life as a man peered out from the shadows on the driver's side. Dark hair swept back from a broodingly handsome face accented by a strong jaw and hollow, raw-boned cheeks. She felt the odd jolt of recognition as the scent of new leather wafted out of the car. Did she know him?

'What's the problem?' he demanded.

Clammy water dripped down inside Cassie's boots and kick-started her tongue—and her indignation.

'You're the problem. Look what you did to me.' She held up her arms to show him the extent of the damage, ruthlessly silencing the zing. He might have a striking face, but his manners sucked.

He swore softly. 'Are you sure that was me?'

The blare of a car horn had Cassie glancing at the lights. Green. 'Of course, I'm sure.'

The horn blared again. Longer and angrier this time.

'I can't stop here.' He straightened back into the shadows and Cassie saw his hand grasp the gear shift.

No way, pal. You are not driving off and leaving me in a puddle on the pavement.

Yanking the heavy door open, she launched herself into the passenger seat.

'Hey!' he said as she slammed the door behind her. 'What the hell do you—?'

'Just drive, Sir Galahad.' She pinned him with her best disgusted look. 'We can discuss your crummy behaviour when you find somewhere to stop.'

His dark brows drew down, the piercing emerald of his irises glittering with annoyance.

'Fine.' He slapped up the indicator, shifted into First. 'But don't drip on the upholstery. This is a rental.'

The car purred to life, and a blast of heat wrapped around Cassie, engulfing her in the subtle aroma of man and leather—and wet velvet. Her heart careered into her throat as the flicker of Selfridges' fairy lights disappeared from her peripheral vision—and the surge of adrenaline that had propelled her into the car smacked head first into her survival instinct.

She was sitting in a complete stranger's car being driven to who knew where—which probably rated a perfect ten on the 'too stupid to live' scale.

'Actually, forget it.' She grasped the door handle.

The driver pulled to a stop at a loading bay. 'So it wasn't me after all.'

Cassie's fingers stilled on the handle at the accusatory tone and her common sense dissolved in a haze of outrage. 'It was definitely you.' She glared at him over the gear shift. 'Don't you know it's Christmas? Show a bit of respect for the season and stop being such a jerk.'

Typical. When Cassie Fitzgerald is on the hunt for a candy man, what does she get? A candy man with a crappy attitude.

Jacob Ryan cranked up the handbrake, slung his arm over the steering wheel and stared at the furious pixie in his passenger seat whose wide violet eyes were shooting daggers at him.

How the hell did I end up with Santa's insane little helper in my car?

As if it weren't bad enough that Helen had manoeuvred him into accepting an invitation to her 'little soirée' tonight, now he had a mad woman in his rented Mercedes. A mad woman who was dripping all over the custom-finished leather upholstery.

He'd never been a fan of the season to be jolly, but this was getting ridiculous.

The sight of the filthy splatter on her coat, though, had the tiniest prickle of guilt surfacing. The car *had* hit a rut in the road.

Hoisting his butt off the seat, he tugged his wallet out of his back pocket. Okay, maybe he had been the culprit. He'd been so aggravated by Helen's petulant demands, he hadn't been paying attention.

'How much?' he asked. A hundred ought to cover it.

Her full Cupid's bow mouth flattened into a grim line and the daggers sharpened. 'I don't want your money,' she announced. 'That's not what this is about.'

Yeah, right.

He counted five crisp twenty-pound notes out of his wallet and presented them to her. 'Here you go. Merry Christmas.'

She gave the money a cursory glance, and the line of her lips twisted into a sneer. 'I told you. I don't want your money, Ebenezer.'

The sarcastic name grated, but then she tightened her arms under her breasts, and his gaze dipped—distracted by the creamy flesh exposed by the wide V in the lapels of her coat.

Hell, is she naked under that thing?

The wayward thought came out of nowhere, and sent a blast of heat somewhere he definitely didn't need it.

'What I want is an apology,' she demanded.

He tore his eyes away from her breasts. 'Huh?'

'An apology? You do know what that is, right?' she said, as if he had an IQ in single figures.

He shook his head, struggling to stem the immature fantasy. Of course she wasn't naked under the coat. Not unless she was a lap dancer. And he doubted that. Given her big doe eyes and the helping of Christmas whimsy she'd dealt him, the picture of her getting sweaty tenners folded into a G-string didn't fit, despite that eye-popping cleavage.

He stuffed the money back into the wallet and dumped it on the dash.

'I apologise,' he said curtly, deciding to humour her.

He didn't usually bother with apologies. Especially to women. Because he'd discovered from experience they didn't count for much. But these were extenuating circumstances. He needed to get her out of the car before that glimpse of cleavage melted the rest of his brain cells and he did something really daft. Like hitting on a crazy lady.

'That's it? That's the best you can do?' She twisted in her seat—all the better to glare at him, he suspected—but the movement made her breasts press against the confines of her coat and threaten to spill out. His mouth went dry.

'I'm going to have to spend an hour on the tube,' she ranted. 'Then get hypothermia walking across the park. And you can't come up with a better—'

'Look, Pollyanna,' he interrupted, the heat tying his gut in knots as he breathed in a lungful of her scent. Cinnamon and cloves and orange. 'I've offered you money and you don't want it,' he ranted right back when she remained silent. 'I apologised and you don't want that, either. Short of sawing off my right arm and gift-wrapping it I don't know what else I'm supposed to do to make amends.'

Her mouth closed and her delicately arched eyebrows launched up her forehead into the soft brown curls that haloed around her head.

That had certainly shut her up. Although he wasn't quite sure what he'd said that had put the shell-shocked look on her face. The unusual colour of her eyes had darkened to a vivid turquoise and all the pigment had leached out of her cheeks.

She covered her mouth with her fingers. 'Jace the Ace.'

The words were muffled, but distinctive enough to make him tense. 'How do you know my name?' he asked, although no one had called him by that particular nickname for fourteen years. Not since he'd been kicked out of school when he was seventeen. The minute the thought registered, another more disturbing one hit him—and the insistent throbbing in his groin increased.

Damn it. That had to be it. What other explanation was there for his instant response to her?

She hadn't replied, so he forced himself to ask the obvious next question.

'Have I slept with you?'

He doesn't remember me. Thank you, God.

Cassie tried to speak, but her tongue was too numb to form coherent words. Not all that surprising given that the punch of recognition had hit her squarely in the solar plexus and expelled all the air from her lungs. She shook her head. 'No,' she whispered.

'I *definitely* didn't sleep with you?' he asked as the unflinching emerald gaze that had broken a thousand female hearts at Hillsdown Road Secondary School searched her face.

She nodded.

His shoulders relaxed and she heard him mutter, 'Good to know.'

No wonder she hadn't recognised him straight away. The Jacob Ryan she remembered had been a boy. A tall, troubled and heart-stoppingly handsome boy, who at seventeen had been the perfect mix of dashing and dangerous to a girl of thirteen with an overactive imagination and hyperactive hormones.

They hadn't slept together. In fact, they'd never even kissed. She'd been four years younger than him, and when you were at school that might as well have been a fifty-year age difference. But she'd had a wealth of immature romantic fantasies about him—like every other girl in her year—which were now playing havoc with her heartbeat.

She shifted in her seat, feeling disorientated and a little light-headed, the damp velvet of her coat like a straightjacket.

Her stomach muscles clenched and released. Exactly as they always had all those years ago, if she'd spied him brooding in the dinner hall, or at the bus shelter busy ignoring all the girls giggling around him... Or during what had come to be known in the annals of Cassie's teenage years as The Ultimate Humiliation. The excruciating moment when she'd disturbed him and head girl Jenny Kelty snogging on the back stairwell.

Cassie's nipples tightened painfully, the impossibly erotic picture they'd made entwined on the dimly lit staircase still astonishingly fresh.

She'd been anchored to the spot, her thigh muscles dissolving as she gawped. His hand had been under Jenny's blouse, his stroking fingers visible beneath the billowing white cotton. Cassie had watched transfixed, her teeth digging into her lip, as his other hand had skimmed to Jenny's waist then moulded her bottom, grinding her against him. Then he'd raised his head and nipped at Jenny's bottom lip. And Cassie had felt her own lip tingle.

As Jenny had groaned and writhed, warmth had flooded through Cassie's system and her strangled gasp had slipped out without warning.

Jace Ryan's sure steady gaze had locked on her face. She'd been trapped, like a deer about to be mown down by a juggernaut. Frozen in terror as reaction skidded up her spine.

But instead of looking angry at the interruption, he had curved his sensual lips into a confidential grin. As if they shared a secret joke that only they understood.

She'd grinned back, opened her mouth to say something, anything.

Then Jenny had spotted her standing there like an idiot and screeched, 'What are you smiling at, you silly cow? Get lost.'

Hot humiliation had blazed through her entire body and she'd scrambled back down the stairs so fast she'd nearly broken her neck. The pounding of blood in her ears far too loud to hear the words Jace shouted after her as she ran.

He turned back to her now, tapped his thumb on the steering wheel. 'So what's your name?'

'Cassie Fitzgerald.'

His forehead furrowed. 'I don't remember anyone called—'

'That's a relief,' she interrupted, praying his memory loss lasted a lifetime. 'That chartreuse blazer was not a good look for me.'

He chuckled. The low rumble of amusement did funny things to her thigh muscles. 'Look, why don't we start over?' he said, his eyes darkening as his gaze rose to the top of her head, then settled back on her face. 'I've got a suite at The Chesterton. Why don't you come back with me? We can get your coat dry-cleaned.' Reaching forward, he tucked a curl behind her ear. 'It's the least I can do for an old school chum.'

They hadn't been chums. Not even close.

'I'm not sure that's a good idea,' she murmured, trying not to pander to the thrum of awareness that pulsed against her cheek where his finger had touched.

Jace Ryan had been dangerous to a woman's peace of mind at seventeen. He was probably deadly now.

He sent her a conspiratorial wink. 'Good is overrated.'

Cassie's pulse sped up, then slowed to a sluggish crawl—and she completely forgot about not pandering to the thrum. 'Is bad better, then?'

He smiled, the penetrating green gaze sweeping over her—and the thrum went haywire.

'In my experience—' his eyes met hers '—bad is not only

better, it's also a lot more fun.' He glanced over his shoulder to check the traffic. 'So how about it?' he asked as the car pulled away from the kerb. 'You want to come back to the hotel and we can raid the mini-bar together while I get your coat cleaned?'

'Okay,' she replied, before she had a chance to think better of it. 'If you're sure it's not too much bother?'

He sent her an easy grin. 'Not at all.'

Crossing her arms, Cassie pressed down on her treacherous boobs, which were still throbbing at the memory of Jace Ryan on that stairwell a million years ago, and studied his profile in the glimmer of the passing streetlights.

Maturity suited him: the light tan, the hint of five o'clock shadow, the thick waves of dark hair, the little lines at the corners of his eyes and the once angry red scar that had faded to a thin white line slashing rakishly across his left eyebrow. He'd grown into those brooding heartthrob features, his hollow cheeks defined to create a dramatic sweep of planes and angles. And from the powerful physique stretching the expertly tailored suit as he shifted gears, he'd also grown into his lanky build.

Cassie huddled in her seat as the powerful car accelerated onto Park Lane. The majestic twenty-foot spruce under Marble Arch glided past, its red and gold star-shaped lights glittering festively in the early winter dusk.

He'd asked her if he'd slept with her—which meant either he suffered from amnesia, or he'd slept with so many women in his time, he couldn't remember the details. Recalling the never-ending string of girlfriends he'd had at Hillsdown Road, Cassie would take a wild guess it was the latter.

Jace Ryan was the sort of guy no sensible woman would ever want to have a relationship with. But as she watched him drive his flashy car with practised efficiency, sexual attraction rippled across her nerve-endings and the thrum of awareness peaked.

Jace Ryan might be a dead loss in the relationship department, but could he be the ultimate candy man? Because as coincidences went, this one was kind of hard to ignore.

She eased out an unsteady breath.

And did she have a sweet enough tooth—and enough guts—to risk taking a lick?

CHAPTER TWO

THAT would be a no, then, came the answer as Cassie peered out the windshield of Jace's car. Evergreen garlands of holly and trailing ivy shimmered with a thousand tiny lights on the ornate stone and gold frontage of the luxury hotel.

When Jace had mentioned The Chesterton she hadn't pictured him having a suite at this art deco palace on Park Lane. The vision of her scurrying into its rarefied elegance in her soiled coat and muddy biker boots plunged her ridiculous candy man fantasy into cold hard reality.

He had offered to get her coat cleaned. He had not offered to perk up her Christmas with prurient sexual favours. And he wasn't likely to when she looked such a fright.

Jace skirted the hood of the car and took the front steps two at a time. He tossed the car keys to a doorman, whose gold-braided green livery and matching top hat weren't doing a thing for Cassie's anxiety levels.

What on earth had she been thinking when she'd accepted his invitation? She felt as if she were thirteen again, getting caught staring at something she shouldn't on that stairwell.

She slid down in the deep bucket seat as the doorman approached the car. Swinging the door open with a slight bow, he sent her a courteous smile.

'It's a pleasure to welcome you to The Chesterton, Ms Fitzgerald.' He held out a hand. 'Mr Ryan has requested we collect your dry-cleaning as soon as you are settled in his suite.'

Cassie stepped out of the car, but studiously avoided letting her coat touch the poor man. Like he wanted mud all over his nice clean uniform. Jace waited at the hotel's revolving doors, looking confident and relaxed and completely at ease in the exclusive surroundings.

She wrapped her arms round her waist as she mounted the steps towards him.

Candy man or not, Jace Ryan was way too much for her to handle. He'd probably known more about seduction when he was seventeen than she ever would. The thrum of awareness that had arched between them had been nothing more than the echo of an old crush. Which she'd grown out of years ago.

She touched his arm before he could direct her through the revolving doors into the lobby.

'Is there a back entrance?' she asked, dropping her hand as her fingers connected with the solid strength beneath the blue silk of his suit.

His lips twitched. 'I wouldn't know. Why?'

'I'm all wet.' Hadn't he noticed she looked like something the cat had dragged through a puddle?

His gaze wandered over her, and the back of her neck burned. 'Your coat took the worst of it. Just take it off.'

She slipped off the wet coat and bunched it in her hands, the blush climbing into her cheeks.

A rueful smile curved his lips and she thought he whispered, 'Pity.'

'Sorry?' Was it her imagination or was there a twinkle of mischief in his eyes?

'Nothing,' he murmured, but the twinkle didn't dim one bit.

The simple sapphire tunic skimmed the top of her thighs and was one of her favourites of Nessa's designs, but the short sleeves and plunging neckline meant wearing it without a coat was a good way to get hypothermia in December. The fragile, bias-cut fabric moulded to her figure as the wind brushed against her skin and made her shiver. She clamped her teeth together to stop them chattering and jumped when his warm palm settled on the small of her back.

'Here.' He shrugged out of his jacket and draped the garment over her shoulders. 'I'll take that.' He lifted her coat out of her arms.

She gripped the lapels of his jacket, the tailored silk dwarfing her as he placed his hand on her hip and led her through the revolving doors into the marble lobby. The fragrance of the roses, freshly cut pine boughs and cinnamon sticks arranged in giant urns by the reception desk greeted them, but did nothing to mask the scent of soap and man that clung to his jacket.

'Wait here.'

Crossing to the desk, he handed over her coat to one of the uniformed receptionists, who took the wet garment without showing a hint of surprise, then sent Cassie an efficient smile. As if it were perfectly normal for half-dressed women to track mud over their foyer.

Cassie tried to look invisible in Jace's jacket as he led her through an ornately furnished lounge accented by deep-seated sofas in tartan upholstery, polished mahogany occasional tables and wrought-iron planters overflowing with winter flora. A scattering of perfectly dressed people sipped afternoon tea from delicate china cups and watched her pass.

Fabulous. She felt like Cinderella arriving at the ball in her rags.

When they stepped into the lift, she eased back against the panelling, still clinging to the jacket. 'This place is seriously posh.'

He huffed out a laugh. 'Don't let them intimidate you.

They're just rich, they're not royalty. Or at least most of them aren't.'

'Fabulous,' she said wryly.

He chuckled again, shoving one hand into his pocket as he stabbed the top button on the display panel. She tried not to notice the way the movement made the linen of his shirt tighten across one broad shoulder.

His gaze took a leisurely trip down to her biker boots and back again as the lift whisked through the floors. She clamped down on the sudden wish to have him like what he saw.

Been there, done that, got the battered ego to prove it.

But when his eyes lifted to her face at last, the beat of anticipation still throbbed in her ears.

'Money doesn't buy you class,' he said. 'I ought to know.'

Sympathy welled and lodged in her throat, the blunt statement reminding her of the angry boy he'd once been. No one had ever found out that much about him at Hillsdown Road, his air of mystery only tantalising his army of admirers more. But one thing she did know was that he'd come from a 'bad home', because she'd overheard Ms Tremall, the head of the sixth form, talking about him to the headmaster, Mr Gates.

'You've got more than enough class to go round now,' she said passionately, the injustice of the teacher's whispered comments surging back. Like all the rest of the school staff, Tremall and Gates had condemned him because of his background and never given him the benefit of the doubt.

His eyebrow arched at her rabble-rousing tone. 'It's not class. It's money,' he said, with more than a hint of irony. 'But I find it does the job just as well.'

The relaxed statement made her feel foolish. Who exactly did she think she was defending here? He certainly wasn't that troubled boy any more. In fact, from his exceedingly posh digs, he was most likely a millionaire. She shook the thought off. Probably best not to go there given her already thriving inferiority complex.

The lift bell pinged and the doors slid back to reveal a marble lobby area only slightly less palatial than the one downstairs.

Here too, a tall vase filled with dark red lilies gave the carved stone and gilded plasterwork a Christmas glow. Using his key card to open a mahogany door, he stood back as she walked into a vaulted hallway that led into a suite of rooms.

Cassie came to an abrupt halt, dismayed by the deep-pile carpeting that led down the corridor into what looked like a large living room.

'Is there a problem?' he asked, lifting the jacket off her shoulders.

'I should take off my boots.' Mud would not look good on all that magnolia.

'Go ahead.' He slung the jacket over a chair. 'I'll call Housekeeping and get them polished while your coat's cooking.'

'That's… Thanks,' she said, embarrassed.

She hopped on one leg to unzip one of the boots, only to jerk upright when he placed his hand on her waist.

'Hold on to my shoulder,' he said casually enough, but as his eyes connected with hers the awareness that prickled up her spine reminded her of that dark school hallway a lifetime ago. Except this time those long, strong fingers held her, and not Jenny Kelty.

'Thanks,' she mumbled, her heartbeat battering her ribcage like a sledgehammer.

She touched his shoulder blade for balance, only to have her insides tilt alarmingly as the muscled sinews tensed beneath her fingers.

He kept his hand on her waist as she struggled with the

boots. But once she'd yanked them off and pulled away from his touch, she realised she had another problem.

'You might want to lose those too,' he mentioned, apparently reading her mind as he examined the wet leggings. 'They're soaked.'

'Right.' She hesitated. The problem was, without her leggings, she'd only have the butt-skimming tunic on. She did a quick mental check. Had she put on her much-prized silk high-leg panties with the lace trim this morning, or had she opted for the usual cheap cotton passion-killers?

The instant the dilemma registered, she yanked herself back to reality.

For pity's sake, Cass. It doesn't matter what knickers you're wearing.

The state of her undies had no bearing whatsoever on this situation. She was here to get her coat cleaned. Nothing more. Bending down, she wiggled out of the leggings and then shoved them under her arm.

'You warm enough?' he asked.

Gripping the hem of the tunic, she yanked it down, goose pimples rising on her bare thighs as her toes curled into the downy-soft carpeting.

'Fine, thanks,' she murmured, noticing the tiny dimple winking in one hard, chiselled cheek. That he found her predicament amusing only confirmed how ludicrous that moment of vanity had been. He wasn't remotely interested in her. Or her knickers.

'Make yourself comfortable in the lounge.' He indicated the large living area as the dimple deepened. 'While I get these sent down.' He picked up her boots, then reached for the leggings under her arm.

She forced herself to relax so he could take them. 'Oh— Okay.' She cleared her throat when the words came out on a squeak. 'Thanks, I will.'

'Help yourself to a drink.' To her dismay he didn't turn, but seemed to be waiting for her to move first. 'They're in the cabinet under the flat-screen.'

She opened her mouth to say thanks for the millionth time, then thought better of it. He'd probably got the message loud and clear by now. Bobbing her head, she forced herself to move. But as she headed towards the lounge, her footsteps silenced by the carpet, she strained to hear him walk away. When silence reined, she couldn't help hoping that if anything was peeping out from under her tunic, it involved crimson lace and not utilitarian white cotton.

Jace spotted the flash of white cotton and the pulse of heat tugged low in his abdomen.

Something about the plain, simple underwear only made the sight more erotic. For a small woman, she certainly had a lot of leg. Slim and well toned, the soft skin of her thighs and calves flushed a delightful shade of pink, making the bright white of her panties all the more striking.

What made his lust a little weird, though, was that he'd remembered her. When those big blue eyes had lifted to his face a moment ago, the flashback had been so strong, he'd known instantly it wasn't a mistake. Or a trick of his libido.

She was the kid who had once disturbed him and one of his girlfriends on the back stairwell at school. He couldn't remember the girlfriend's name, couldn't even picture her face. All he really remembered about her was that she'd been more than willing and she hadn't had much of a sense of humour, which was why he'd dropped her like a stone after she'd shouted at the child watching them and scared her off.

But he could see Cassie Fitzgerald clearly enough. He'd been kicked out of school two days later, and the memory had quickly become buried amid all the crap he'd had to deal with when he'd been expelled.

But the image of her heart-shaped face came back to him now with surprising clarity.

She'd been young, way too young for him and not conventionally pretty. Those bewitching eyes had been too large for her face and her wide lips at the time had seemed too full. He hadn't fancied her, not in the least. She had been a baby. But something about the way she'd been watching him had struck a chord. Those big eyes of hers had grown huge in her face, and he'd felt as if she could see right into his soul, but, unlike everyone else, she hadn't been judging him. He'd smiled, because she'd looked so shocked, and it had been funny, but also because, for a second, he'd forgotten to feel jaded and angry and resentful, forgotten even his burning quest to get Miss No-Name's bra off and instead had felt like a kid again himself.

Unfortunately, as Cassie Fitzgerald disappeared into the lounge and the flash of white cotton disappeared with her, she wasn't making him feel like a kid any more. Not now that little girl had grown up—and into her unusual beauty.

Squeezing the damp fabric of her leggings in his fist, he lifted them to his nose, breathed in the sultry, Christmassy scent of cinnamon and oranges, only slightly masked by the earthy smell of rain-water, that had got to him in the car—and realised he was in serious trouble.

The impromptu decision to invite her to his suite had seemed like a good idea at the time. He had an hour to kill before he had to turn up at Helen's soirée and convince her once and for all to leave him alone, and he didn't want to think about what a pain in the backside that was going to be. Cassie would provide a welcome distraction. Plus getting her coat cleaned had solved the mystery of what it was she did or did not have on under it.

But he hadn't expected her to be quite this distracting. Her skittishness as soon as they'd arrived at the hotel had intrigued him. And the way she'd defended him in the lift had surprised the hell out of him—and reminded him of that kid on the stairwell. But what was distracting him a whole lot more was the sight of her lush, curvaceous figure in that dress, which was roughly the size of a place mat, and the resulting shot of arousal currently pounding like a sore tooth in his groin.

Not only was he going to find it next to impossible to keep his hands off her for the forty minutes the receptionist had said it would take to clean her clothing.

He was fast losing the will to even try.

Which was annoying. Mindless, meaningless sex had lost its appeal a long time ago—and he didn't seduce women he'd only just met any more.

Only problem was, right now, he couldn't for the life of him remember why.

Cassie stood by the wall of panelled glass, spellbound as she gazed out over the wraparound roof terrace and the dark expanse of Hyde Park below, the fairground lights of the Winter Wonderland shimmering playfully in the distance. She sipped from the glass of Merlot she'd poured herself to ease her dry throat, then placed it on a smooth walnut coffee table. She must be careful not to drink it all. Not only was it still barely six o'clock, but she'd forgotten to ask her host how long her clothes would take—so she didn't know how long she would be required to keep her wits about her. She'd always been a very cheap drunk. And on the evidence of her recent knicker meltdown, dulling her wits with alcohol could well lead to more candy man fantasies. Which was the last thing she needed if she didn't want to make this more awkward than it already was. Better to stay sober and sensible.

Swivelling round, she took in the full grandeur of Jace Ryan's hotel suite. Then released a staggered breath. This was the penthouse suite—the lofty view of Hyde Park nothing short of spectacular. The lounge area alone was considerably larger than her entire flat. She set aside her apprehension about spending time in his company as curiosity about him burned. How had the angry youth from a 'bad home' who'd been summarily expelled from their bog-standard comprehensive fourteen short years ago ended up affording the best suite in one of London's best hotels? Had he robbed a bank or something?

'Right, we're all set.' The man in question strolled into the room and dumped his key card on the coffee table next to her glass of wine. Even in the tailored trousers and linen shirt, he could easily be a bank robber, Cassie thought. He certainly had that confident, dangerous edge that made him seem capable of anything.

He delved into the bar and came up with a bottle of imported Italian beer. 'Do you need a top-up?' he asked, nodding towards her glass as he twisted off the bottle cap.

He'd rolled up his shirt sleeves, revealing forearms roped with muscle as he took a long slug of the beer.

'No, thanks,' she said. A couple of sips would definitely have to be her limit. 'Do you know how long the dry-cleaning will take?'

He shrugged. 'About forty minutes,' he said, sinking into one of the leather sofas. 'Take a seat.' He signalled the cushions next to him with his bottle, then kicked off his loafers and propped his stockinged feet on the table. 'You might as well get comfortable.'

Not likely, given that the sight of him lounging on his sofa was making her pulse pound like a timpani drum. He looked like a male supermodel, for goodness' sake, with those long, leanly muscled legs displayed in perfectly creased trousers, the rugged shadow of stubble on his chin, and his dark hair sexily mussed.

Forget candy man… Jace Ryan was an entire sweetshop.

She sat gingerly on the sofa opposite him, not about to risk getting too close to all that industrial-strength testosterone. Swooning would not be good.

Her tunic rose up her thighs and she hastily shifted onto her bottom, tucking her legs up under her to hide any hint of plain white cotton from view. If he looked like a supermodel, she looked like a banner ad for dull and boring.

She tore her eyes away from the intensity of his gaze, which seemed to have zeroed in on her face.

'How did you do it?' she asked, struggling to think of a safe topic for small talk.

'Do what?'

The puzzled reply had her realising the gaucheness of the question. 'I just wondered how you…' She trailed off, wishing she'd never asked. Was he embarrassed by his past? She doubted it. Sitting in the midst of the luxury he'd earned, he looked perfectly at home. Even so, she didn't want to pry.

'How did I manage to afford all this?' he prompted.

She debated trying to pretend she'd been asking something else, but had to give up on the idea. She couldn't think of an alternative interpretation. And even if she could, the steady, knowing look in his eyes suggested he already knew exactly what she'd been referring to.

She nodded, and took one more sip of wine, strictly for Dutch courage purposes.

He tilted his head to one side, as if considering his answer. 'I discovered I had a talent for design.' He paused for less than a heartbeat, but she heard the hesitation. 'Or rather my parole officer discovered I had a talent for design.'

'Your parole officer?' she asked, startled. He *had* robbed a bank.

'Relax.' He grinned, the light in his eyes twinkling again. 'It's all right. I'm not an ex-con.'

'I didn't think you were,' she lied.

'He was a young-offenders liaison officer. The school pressed charges. After they expelled me.'

'But that's ridiculous. The drawings were hilarious.' She could still remember the reason he'd been expelled. And the pinpoint accuracy of the staff caricatures he'd graffiti'd all over the back wall of the new gym in DayGlo spray paint.

'Gates never did have a sense of humour.' Jace shrugged. 'And it worked out fine for me.' Again she heard the slight hesitation. 'I got to move into a bedsit and onto an art foundation course—thanks to the officer assigned to my case, who actually believed I could be rehabilitated.'

'But you didn't need rehabilitating. You just needed someone to believe in you.'

His lips quirked in an indulgent smile. 'You really are Pollyanna, aren't you?'

'It's not that, it's just…' *What?* 'You didn't deserve to be treated so harshly. It was only a bit of fun.'

He placed his bottle on the table. 'It was criminal damage. And it wasn't the first time. So of course I deserved it.' The smile stayed in place, as if it didn't matter in the slightest. 'But that's more than enough about me.' He took his feet off the table, leaned forward and rested his elbows on his knees. 'Let's talk about you. You're much more interesting.'

'Me?' She pressed her hand to her chest. Was he kidding? 'Believe me, I'm not as interesting as you.'

'I'll be the judge of that.' He lifted his beer, held it poised at his mouth and studied her with an intensity that made her breath catch. 'So is Cassie short for Cassandra?' He took a swig and her eyes dipped involuntarily to the sensual line of his lips. He lowered the bottle. 'Apollo's paramour,' he murmured. 'Gifted with the power of prophecy but forever cursed not to be believed.'

Cassie trembled, the rough cadence of his voice sending

little shivers of excitement over her skin. She gave a breathless laugh, her gaze darting back to his face. 'If only it were that exciting.'

His lips edged into a seductive smile. 'It's not exciting. Cassandra's story is tragic.'

Not from where I'm sitting.

Cassie smiled despite the tension that crackled in the air. Was he trying to melt her into a puddle of lust? Or was that just wishful thinking on her part? 'Cassie's short for Cassidy.'

His eyebrow rose a fraction. 'Cassidy?'

'As in David Cassidy,' Cassie added, her grin spreading as his eyebrow arched upwards. 'The seventies teen idol. Unfortunately my mum was a huge fan. And I've been suffering ever since.'

How fitting that her mum had given her a name as unsexy as her knickers.

'Mind you, it could have been worse,' she continued, amused by his obvious surprise. 'Thank God she wasn't a Donny Osmond fan or I would have been saddled with Ossie.'

His laugh rumbled out, low and rough and setting off the little shivers again. 'I like Cassidy. It's unusual. Which suits you.'

She tipped her glass up in a toast. 'Yup, that's me, very unusual.' *If only.* 'Unlike you. Who's so totally run of the mill,' she added, unable to resist fluttering her eyelashes.

Instead of looking appalled at her heavy-handed attempt at flirtation, he clinked his bottle against her glass. 'You are unusual,' he said. 'Why don't you believe me?'

She took another hasty sip. The rich, heady wine flowed down her throat and wrapped around her chest like a winter quilt.

She let her gaze wander over to the blue spruce expertly decorated with glass baubles and ribbon bows in the corner. Jace Ryan might be a lot more man than she felt capable of handling. But where was the harm in enjoying his company? At least for as long as it took to clean her coat.

'How exactly am I unusual?' she asked, knowing it wasn't true, but happy to have him try to persuade her.

He placed his beer bottle on the coffee table and stood up. Lifting her hand from her lap, he wrapped his long fingers around it and gave a soft tug to pull her off the sofa. 'Stand up, so we can examine the evidence.'

She did as she was told, the appreciative gleam as his gaze roamed over her shocking her into silence.

'Your eyes are a really unusual colour. I noticed that as soon as you jumped into my car. Even though you were ruining the upholstery and calling me a jerk.'

'I only called you a jerk because you were being a jerk,' she pointed out in her defence.

He placed his hands on her hips. 'Stop ruining the mood.'

'What mood?' she asked, standing so close to him now, she could see the gold flecks in his irises.

The buckle on his belt brushed against her tummy and the little shivers became shock waves, shuddering down to the place between her thighs.

'The mood I'm trying to create' he said, a lock of dark hair flopping over his brow. 'So I can kiss you.'

Her gaze dipped to his mouth, those sensual lips that had once devoured Jenny temptingly close. 'You want to kiss me?' she said on a ragged breath.

He pressed his thumb to her bottom lip, the touch making it tingle. 'I must be seriously losing my touch. Isn't it obvious?'

'But we've only just met,' she whispered, not sure how to respond to his teasing. Did he seriously plan to kiss her? And why the heck was she arguing with him about it?

He wrapped his hand round her waist, pulled her flush

against him. 'Not true,' he remarked, his lips only centimetres from hers. 'We've known each other since school.'

'But you don't remember me.'

'Sure I do.' His warm breath feathered against her cheek. 'You're the little voyeur on the stairwell.'

She tensed and drew back. 'You remember? But how?'

'I told you, those eyes are very unusual.' His lips curved, in that same offhand grin that had captivated her over a decade ago. And suddenly, she understood. This wasn't a seduction. He was making fun of her.

She placed her hands on his chest, stumbled back, the sweet, heady buzz of flirtation and arousal replaced by embarrassment. 'I should go.'

He caught her elbow as she stepped back. 'Hey? What's the rush all of a sudden?'

'I just...I have to go,' she mumbled, pulling her arm free.

'Don't be ridiculous—your coat isn't back yet.'

She tugged down the hem of her tunic, feeling hideously exposed.

'I'll wait downstairs, in the lobby.' It would be mortifying in her bare feet, but what could be more mortifying than simpering all over a guy who was secretly laughing at her?

She crossed the living room, holding her head up.

'Hang on a minute. You're being absurd. What exactly are you so upset about?'

The frustrated words stopped her dead. She swung round.

He stood by his walnut coffee table, looking like a poster boy for original sin and the humiliation coalesced in her stomach into a hot ball of resentment.

'I know I'm absurd,' she said, and watched his brow crease in a puzzled frown. 'I had a massive crush on you. Which was my own stupid fault. I admit it.' She walked back and poked him in the chest. 'But that doesn't give you the right to make fun of me. Now or then.'

He grasped her finger, the green of his irises darkening to a stormy emerald. 'I'm not making fun of you. And I didn't then.'

'Yes, you did.' She tugged her finger free, not liking the way his touch had set off those silly shivers again. 'I heard you and Jenny Kelty laughing at me.' Not that it mattered now, but it was the principle of the thing. She had gone over that encounter a thousand times in her mind in the months that followed. And felt more and more mortified every time. Why had she stood there like a lemon? Why had she smiled at him? But she could see now, she hadn't been the only one at fault. They shouldn't have laughed at her.

'Who the hell is Jenny Kelty?' he asked.

'Unbelievable,' she said, exasperated. 'Don't you remember any of the girls you slept with back then either?'

'It was a long time ago.' He shoved his fingers through his hair, the movement jerky and a lot less relaxed than before. 'And whatever her name was, I didn't sleep with her. You put a stop to that.'

'Well, good,' she said, righteous indignation framing each word. 'I'm glad I saved Jenny from becoming yet another notch on your bedpost.'

'You didn't save Jenny. She saved herself. Once I found out what a cow she was, my interest in her cooled considerably.'

Jenny *had* been a cow, and every girl foolish enough to cross her had known it, but Cassie was still startled by the vehemence in the statement.

'So what changed your mind about Jenny?' She threw the words back at him. 'Did she refuse to snog you?'

His eyebrows rose another notch at the sarcastic tone. And Cassie felt power surge through her veins as if she had been plugged into a nuclear reactor.

Finally she, Cassie Fitzgerald, was standing up for herself.

And not letting her rose-tinted glasses blind her to the truth. She wasn't dumb little Cassie who had caught her fiancée on the couch with his lover and was too stupid to see it coming. Or naive little Cassie who felt pathetically grateful just because a sexy guy had said her eyes were an unusual colour and that he wanted to kiss her. She was bold, brash, powerful Cassie, prepared to fight for the respect and consideration she deserved.

'She didn't refuse to snog me,' he said easily. 'I refused to snog her. After she shouted at you and scared the hell out of you.'

'I—' The tirade she'd planned cut off. 'After she what?'

'I don't like bullies and I told her so.' He slung a hand into the pocket of his trousers. 'She got the hump and stomped off. And I was glad to see the back of her.'

'But you...' That couldn't be right. That wasn't how she remembered the incident at all. 'But you were laughing at me, too. I heard you.' Hadn't she?

He shrugged. 'I very much doubt that, as I didn't find her behaviour remotely funny.'

'But I thought...' Cassie trailed off, the power surge deflating inside her like a popped party balloon. 'I misunderstood.'

He'd stood up for her. The knowledge should have pleased her. But it didn't. It only made her feel more idiotic.

How come she'd instantly assumed he hadn't stood up for her? Why had her self-esteem been so low? Even then? And why on earth had she flown off the handle like that about a minor incident that had happened years ago? And meant absolutely nothing?

He probably thought she was a complete nutjob.

She risked a glance at him. But instead of looking concerned at the state of her mental health, he looked amused, that damn sexy grin bringing out the dimple in his cheek.

'Now we've cleared that up,' he said, 'why don't you sit back down and finish your wine?'

Wine was probably the last thing she needed, but doing what he suggested seemed easier than getting into a debate about what a complete twit she'd made of herself.

She perched on the edge of the sofa and lifted the glass to her lips, another even more dismal thought occurring to her. He really had been planning to kiss her. But there was no chance he'd want to kiss her now.

Nice one, Cass.

He picked up his bottle and saluted her. 'So let's talk about that massive crush.'

She sucked in a surprised breath at the bold statement, inhaled wine instead of air and choked.

CHAPTER THREE

JACE rose and stepped over the coffee table as his guest coughed and sputtered. Settling beside her, he gave her a hefty pat on the back. 'Take a breath.'

The coughing stopped as Cassie drew air into her lungs and cast a wary look over her shoulder. She shuddered as he ran his palm up her back, exploring the delicate bumps of her spine beneath the skimpy dress.

Either she was the most fascinating woman he'd ever met or she was totally nuts, but either way she was proving to be one hell of a diversion. And her little temper tantrum had only intrigued him more.

He'd never met anyone before whose every emotion was so plainly written on their face.

He'd been accused of worse things in his time...most of which he had actually done, so, rather than feeling aggrieved at her accusations, he was oddly flattered that moment on the stairwell had mattered to her so much. And quietly astonished to discover at least one incident from his teenage years when he'd actually done the right thing. Given that his schooldays had sped past in a maelstrom of bad behaviour and even worse choices, that was no small feat.

'The wine went down the wrong way,' she said, straightening away from his touch.

He plucked a tissue out of the dispenser on the coffee table, and handed it to her. 'Now about that massive crush?'

She sent him a quelling look, but the pretty little flags of colour that appeared in her cheeks contradicted it. 'I don't think your ego needs that kind of validation,' she said so cautiously, his lips twitched.

'Probably not.' He settled back, stretched his arms across the sofa cushions, and noted that she was now perched so precariously on the edge of her seat it was a wonder she hadn't toppled onto the floor. He was used to women throwing themselves at him, so the fact that he found her wariness refreshing was probably a bit perverse. 'But I've got to admit I'm fascinated. Weren't you a little young to have a massive crush on me?'

'I was thirteen,' she said, the tantalising sparkle of annoyance returning to her eyes.

'Oh, right. Thirteen. An old woman, then,' he teased.

'I was in love.' She frowned slightly, reconsidering the implications of the statement. 'Or at least I thought I was. At the time.'

'Is that a cryptic way of saying you haven't got a massive crush on me any more?'

Her stern expression cracked a little. 'You covered me in dirty water, then tried to deny it. Do I look like a masochist?'

Leaning forward, he skimmed a knuckle down her cheek. 'For the record, it was an accident. And I did eventually see the error of my ways.'

Her gaze skittered away, but this time she didn't shift out of reach. 'Tell me something,' she said softly. 'Do you try to kiss every woman you meet?'

He smiled. Nuts or not, her candour was captivating. 'The answer is no.' Sitting up, he nudged the riotous curls of chestnut hair over her shoulder. 'Not *every* woman.'

Her gaze came back to his and her throaty chuckle made

reaction coil in his gut. 'You must have kissed quite a few, though, if you can't remember who they are.'

He stifled a groan. Busted. 'What can I say? I had a misspent youth.'

He'd been reckless and easily bored as a teenager and had found it far too convenient to seduce women and then forget about them. Not something he was all that proud of now. But he'd eventually realised, like most hormonally charged boys when they became men, that quality was much more rewarding than quantity. And that women deserved to be savoured. And Cassie Fitzgerald was fast becoming a woman he definitely planned to savour. The only problem was, he didn't want to rush her and risk scaring her off.

'If it's any consolation…' he looped his finger in one of her curls, watched the silky hair spring back against her cheek '…I can guarantee you, I pay a lot more attention now.'

Her tongue flicked out to moisten her lips and he felt the jolt right down to his toes.

'We could always give it another go,' she said, a tentative smile lifting one corner of that lush mouth. 'If you want.'

'That sounds like a plan,' he murmured.

Caressing her nape, he threaded his fingers through the tendrils of hair then slanted his lips across hers. He wasn't going to wait for a second invitation.

Cassie braced her palms against his chest as his mouth captured hers. His lips were firm, hot, demanding. His pectoral muscles flexed beneath his shirt as he angled his head to deepen the kiss.

Heat scalded the pit of her stomach and radiated out, sizzling and tingling across her skin. He raised his other hand, massaged her scalp to hold her in place. She gasped as reaction raced through her, and his tongue thrust into her mouth, exploring in intimate strokes.

She clung on, poised over him as they sank into the sofa cushions—and desire spiralled and twisted inside her. It had been so long since she'd had a chance to feel a man's heat, his mouth on hers, the hardness of his chest pressing into her breasts. And she certainly didn't remember a kiss ever feeling this incredible.

He lifted her head, nipped her bottom lip as he stared into her eyes. His hands cradled her cheeks, his quick smile making the pulse of desire settle lower.

'Thanks, I enjoyed that,' he said, his voice husky. 'It's been a while.'

'For me too,' she said, although she didn't believe him. Anyone who kissed as well as he did had to practise regularly. 'I've wanted to do that ever since I saw you kiss Jenny.'

He stroked her cheek, pressed his thumb into her bottom lip. 'Have you really?'

She sat up. Why had she told him that? Talk about sad.

He skimmed his palm up her bare leg. 'So did I live up to expectations?'

She nodded, not wanting to divulge exactly how strongly the simple kiss had affected her. It would only make her look more sad and pathetic.

'Unfortunately I have an engagement...' He lifted his hand to glance at his wristwatch. 'In about half an hour. Otherwise we could take this further.'

'That's okay.' She should have been relieved. He was letting her down gently. But she didn't feel relieved, she felt disappointed. What had he meant by 'take this further'? How much further?

He shifted, his hand resting back on her thigh, stroking lazily. 'You could wait here until I get back,' he said, the heavy-lidded gaze as arousing as the feel of his rough palm on her skin. 'Although you might get bored.' His fingers slipped under the hem of her tunic, and she shuddered. He laughed. 'And I wouldn't want that.'

Bored? How could she be bored when her body felt as if it were about to explode? 'I don't underst—'

'Or you could come with me,' he interrupted.

Her breath gushed out. She tried to concentrate on what he was saying but it was next to impossible as the tips of his fingers drew lazy circles on her leg. Her sex throbbed, ached, begging for him to move higher still and stroke her there.

'Where to?' she heard herself ask as she tried to keep up her end of the conversation.

'The Blue Tower Restaurant,' he murmured, mentioning London's newest hot spot. His thumb traced the edge of her panties, then dipped underneath and her breath sawed out in a ragged pant.

Her hands fell to his shoulders, and she dug her fingers into the ridge of muscle, scared she was going to fall off the sofa. His green eyes watched her, the lids at half mast.

'I don't...' She swayed towards him. What was happening? What were they talking about? Her skin flushed hot, then cold, then hot again.

His tongue licked at her lips, then he cupped her head, his mouth taking hers in another mind-numbing kiss. Her heavy breasts flattened against the solid wall of his chest, the nipples squeezing into rigid, arching peaks.

'Say yes, Cassie,' he murmured as his fingers eased under the gusset of her panties and plunged.

'Yes.' The single word burst out of her mouth.

'God, you're so wet.' He circled and rubbed her swollen flesh, pushed inside her, his thumb pressing against her clitoris. 'You feel incredible.'

She straddled him, her knees digging into the sofa, her arms wrapping around his shoulders as his fingers continued to drive her into a frenzy. She couldn't talk, couldn't think, couldn't breathe. All thought, all feeling concentrated on the nub of pleasure between her legs. The rigid length of him, confined by his clothing, nudged the inside of her thigh—and she rubbed herself against him, yearning to have him deep inside her.

Her head dropped back and she moaned, heat soaring up her body. 'Please, don't stop.'

His strained laugh brushed against her cheek. 'I'm not going to stop.'

And he didn't, as the spasms of an unstoppable climax eddied up from her toes, coursed through her body and collided in her sex.

'Let go, Cassie. Come for me.'

The orgasm roared through her, exploding into a billion glittering sparks like a firework display on Bonfire Night. She heard someone cry out as the wave of pleasure crashed over her. Someone who sounded a lot like her but was thousands of miles away.

Then she buried her face in his neck, dazed and delirious, and whispered, 'Candy man.'

CHAPTER FOUR

'WHAT did you call me?' At Jace's gruff chuckle, Cassie stiffened and rose to see the teasing grin on his face.

Had she just said that out loud?

'It sounded like candy man,' he added.

'Did it?' She hedged, pressing her palms to the heat in her cheeks.

He laughed. 'Interesting,' he murmured, the smile more than a little smug. 'What does it mean?'

She climbed off his lap, adjusted her clothing, struggling to think straight while noticing the impressive bulge in his trousers. She smoothed the tunic down. 'It means, that was...' She halted, her face flushing. How did you thank a guy for giving you the most incredible orgasm of your life? She'd never come that quickly before, or with such intensity. And certainly not with a man she hadn't been in a relationship with. 'It means, that was amazing. So thanks,' she said, opting for honesty while her endorphins were still high on the afterglow.

He stretched out his arms across the back of the sofa. 'The pleasure's all mine.'

'I'm sorry, you didn't...' Her gaze snagged on his obvious state of arousal, and she wondered if she should offer to do something for him in return. It seemed only fair. 'Would you like me...?'

He tucked a finger under her chin, lifted her gaze to his. 'It's okay, Cassie. I'm not fifteen any more. I can wait.' He placed a quick kiss on her nose, before standing up. 'In fact, unfortunately, we're both going to have to wait, we're already fashionably late.'

'Late? Late for what?'

Instead of answering, he took her hands in his, and hauled her off the sofa. 'If you want to go do whatever it is girls do while they hog the bathroom, go ahead.' He placed his hand on her bottom and gave her a proprietary pat. 'It's that way.'

'Yes, but...where are we going?' she asked, trying to maintain a little sanity. Why had the invitation turned the afterglow into a giddy rush of pleasure?

He settled his hands on her shoulders, swept her hair back and kissed her neck. 'The Blue Tower. With me. This evening.'

When had she agreed to that? 'But I...' She trailed off, unable to concentrate on anything but his lips nuzzling the sensitive skin under her ear—and the darts of sensation shivering down her spine.

The doorbell buzzed and he nipped her ear lobe. 'That'll be your clothes. Don't take too long—we don't want to be too fashionable.' So saying, he strode out of the room.

Locating her bag under the coffee table, Cassie dashed off to the bathroom he'd indicated. She knew when she was being railroaded. But right now she didn't care. She needed time to think.

Once inside the lavish marble bathroom, she flung her bag on the vanity and studied herself in the mirror that covered one wall.

She hardly recognised herself.

Her hair sprung out in all directions, the unruly curls spilling out of the topknot she'd swept it up in that morning. Her cheeks were flushed a vivid red, her lips puffy and swollen, and her pupils so dilated her blue eyes were almost black. She touched her fingertips to the raw spot beneath her bottom lip. And she had whisker burn on her chin.

She looked like a woman who had been well and truly satisfied. She huffed out a breath. Probably because she had been. But she needed to take stock and think clearly now.

Or at least try to think clearly with her brain still addled from the endorphin rush and her core still throbbing from Jace Ryan's exceptionally skilled caresses.

Unwrapping a bar of the fragrant vanilla soap in a basket on the vanity, she washed her hands and face, then doused her cheeks in cold water. After patting herself dry with one of the hotel's monogrammed towels and finger-combing her hair, she examined her face again. She still looked dazed and dishevelled, but at least the colour in her cheeks had subsided from a vivid magenta to a pale rose. And her pupils had shrunk enough so she didn't look as if she were on crack.

Okay, so what had happened out there? She simply wasn't that into sex. Not that she was frigid or anything. She liked sex well enough. The sensible, comforting, predictable kind with a man she knew well and cared about and respected. Even if it later turned out he didn't deserve it. A line formed on her brow in the mirror. However, she did not do the hot, wild, knock-you-for-six kind of sex with a man who was a virtual stranger.

But there was no denying she'd done just that with Jace Ryan.

One minute they'd been talking, then they'd been kissing and then she'd been begging him to bring her to the most earth-shattering orgasm of her life. Another line appeared on her brow. And he had.

How had he known just how to touch her, and where? How had he known so instinctively just what she needed when she didn't know herself? She'd only had two serious boyfriends in her life. Two men whom she'd become sexually intimate with before she'd leapt into Jace Ryan's car this afternoon. She'd known both of them for weeks, months even, before she'd ever considered taking things to the next stage. But even after forming proper committed relationships with them, even after convincing herself she was in love with them, neither of them had ever been able to make her lose her mind as Jace had with a simple touch. In fact, Lance and David, her college boyfriend, had both complained at one time or another that she thought too much during sex, that she wasn't spontaneous enough.

She swallowed heavily, her throat dry. She hadn't merely been spontaneous on Jace's sofa. She'd come close to spontaneously combusting.

And she hadn't been thinking either. In fact, she'd been doing the opposite. Jace had offered to get her coat cleaned, and, less than an hour after walking into his hotel suite, she'd been straddling his thighs and writhing under his touch like a woman possessed. What had happened to her smart, safe, sensible, measured approach to sex and intimacy?

Opening her bag on the vanity, she rummaged for her phone. Unlocking the keypad, she scrolled down to Nessa's name.

What she needed now was some expert advice. Until Nessa had finally admitted that their old school friend Terrence was the love of her life, she'd had an enviably straightforward attitude to men and sex. Nessa knew how to handle a candy man, because, to hear Nessa tell it, she'd had more than her fair share of them.

There was little doubt that Jace Ryan was a candy man. But now she'd identified him, Cassie didn't have a clue what to do with him. Should she do what her hormones were begging her to do? Go out with him this evening so they could finish what they'd started later tonight? Or should she do what her head was telling her and run a mile? Not just from him but from the wild woman who had inhabited her body?

Nessa owed her, she thought as she pressed Dial and listened to the phone ring. It was Nessa's fault she was in this ridiculous situation. If she had kept her advice to herself, Cassie would never have had that moment of recklessness and accepted Jace's invitation in the first place—and ended up having an out-of-body experience on his sofa.

'It's Ness. What's up?' Her friend's familiar greeting had the tension in Cassie's shoulders easing.

'Ness, it's me,' she whispered into the phone. 'I'm in trouble.'

'What kind of trouble?' Nessa replied, her voice instantly direct and focused, reminding Cassie why Nessa was the perfect person to turn to in a crisis.

'Do you remember Jacob Ryan? From school?'

There was a slight pause on the line, then Nessa gave an appreciative purr. 'Oh, yeah. Jace the Ace. That boy's tight white buns looked so fine in black jeans, they occupy a real special place in my school memories. Why?'

'I met him. Tonight. I'm in his bathroom at The Chesterton. And we just had…well, not exactly sex, but nearly sex on his sofa.'

'Define nearly sex?' Nessa said, apparently completely unfazed by Cassie's confession.

'I had an orgasm. A really amazing orgasm,' Cassie blurted out, not quite comfortable discussing the mechanics. 'But he didn't.'

'That's not nearly sex, honey.' Nessa's deep, satisfied laugh echoed down the phone line. 'So little Cassie finally found herself a candy man. I always knew that boy looked fine for a reason.'

'Don't you dare mention that stupid candy-man thing again. I'm in trouble. And you've got to get me out of it.'

'Sounds like good trouble to me.'

'He's asked me to go out with him. Tonight,' Cassie continued, deciding to ignore Nessa's observation. 'To some do at the Blue Tower.' Her lips pursed. Some do that she knew nothing about, because he'd been deliberately cagey with details. 'On the understanding that when we get back, we'll take this further.' She swallowed as her stomach did a back flip. 'A lot further.'

'And you don't want to go further?' Nessa asked.

'It's not that I don't want to.' She did want to—the warm, liquid pull in the pit of her tummy was pretty incriminating on that score. 'I just don't know if I should. I've never had a one-night stand before. And what if he wants more than a one-night stand? I'm not ready for another relationship. Especially not with a guy who—'

'Cass, stop right there. You're overthinking this thing. The question is, did he give you a good time?'

'Yes, but—'

'But nothing,' Nessa interrupted. 'You had a good time. Next question. Is he pressuring you to do the same for him? 'Cos you shouldn't feel beholden.'

Did she feel pressured? Beholden? He'd bulldozed her into agreeing to go to the trendy restaurant, but he'd seemed remarkably relaxed about the sex part of the equation. Even though he'd been fully erect, he hadn't insisted she do anything about it. Her stomach somersaulted at the thought of that long, thick ridge stretching the loose pleats in his trousers. The truth was, if he had insisted, he wouldn't have had to insist very hard.

'No, I guess not.'

'Fine. So what exactly is the problem here? He's given you an amazing orgasm, there's the promise of more and he isn't making you do a thing you don't want to.'

'You don't understand. The problem's not him. It's me. I

don't know what got into me. One minute he was kissing me and the next I was… I lost control. It was like I couldn't stop myself. And it happened so fast. I've never felt like that before. It was scary.'

Nessa's low chuckle didn't do a thing to calm Cassie's nerves. 'Welcome to the club.'

'What club?'

'The Really Amazing Sex Club. It's way past time you got your membership.'

'But how can it have been really amazing when he's a stranger?'

'Because sometimes it's just about the sex,' Nessa said bluntly. 'You've got the urge, he's got the urge. You're both young, free and single and the chemistry's hot. Sometimes it doesn't have to be about anything more than that.'

The loud rap on the door had Cassie juggling the phone.

'Cassie, your time's up.' She heard his low voice through the door and it set off a whole new set of tingles.

'That's him now,' she hissed into the phone. 'Just a sec,' she shouted back. 'I'm doing my make-up.'

'I've got your clothes.'

She whipped the phone behind her back as the door opened. He'd changed out of his suit into a black sweater with a crew neck and dark blue jeans, his tall, broad-shouldered frame filling the doorway. He'd also shaved. Without the five o'clock shadow the line of his jaw looked clean and sharp and the dimple in his cheek more pronounced. His damp hair swept back from his forehead, and the dark waves glistened in the overhead light as he placed her folded coat on the vanity unit with a small bag bearing the logo of an exclusive boutique. 'Your coat. The boots are outside. They couldn't launder the leggings in time so I ordered a replacement.' His smile widened as his gaze inched down her bare legs. 'The car will be here in five.'

'Wait,' she said as he turned to leave. 'How dressy is this do? And whose do is it? Will they mind if I come? I haven't been invited.'

A sensual smile spread across his lips that had her fingers tightening on the phone. '*I'm* inviting you.' Reaching forward, he brushed his thumb across her chin, pressed a quick, sizzling kiss to her lips. She breathed in the clean scent of soap and the spicy hint of aftershave as he raised his head and the pull in her tummy became a yank. 'And you're dressy enough.'

She released the breath as he walked out of the room. Only once the door had closed did she realise he hadn't answered a single one of her questions.

She heard the crackle of Nessa's voice, lifted the phone to her ear.

'I think I just agreed to go,' she murmured, terror and excitement churning in her gut.

Nessa gave a jubilant whoop. 'Don't sound so worried, honey. All you've got to do now is relax, enjoy, flirt your heart out and let your candy man introduce you to all the club's member benefits.'

After bidding Nessa goodbye, Cassie disconnected the phone and shoved it back in her bag.

She dug her emergency make-up out, and counted to ten to stop herself from hyperventilating as she took the top off her liquid eyeliner.

Relax. Enjoy. Flirt. She could do that. How hard could it be?

But as she hastily lined her bottom lid with black kohl her fingers were trembling so hard, she nearly poked her eye out.

CHAPTER FIVE

CASSIE focused on evening out her breathing as the chauffeur-driven car pulled away from the kerb and the lights of The Chesterton blurred behind them. Going out on the town with a devastatingly sexy guy to one of London's hottest night-spots was exactly what she needed to dynamite herself out of her pre-Christmas funk. And getting to do it in serious style was not going to intimidate her.

She shouldn't over-analyse this situation and second-guess her behaviour. Her confidence had taken a huge knock when she'd walked in on Lance and Tracy. He hadn't been faithful to her, and she'd thought she'd moved on. But the truth was a tiny part of her had always blamed herself. She hadn't done enough, been exciting enough to keep him interested. And that nasty little seed had festered ever since, making her doubt herself. Tonight would be about getting that part of herself back. And moving on in body as well as spirit.

A warm palm came to rest on her leg. Jace rubbed his thumb across her kneecap and she trembled, the heat seeping through the luxury silk he'd ordered to replace her wet leggings.

'We won't stay long. There's no need to be nervous.'

His dark gaze devoured her, the promise in his eyes so compelling nervous energy turned into the sharp tug of sexual arousal.

'I'm not nervous,' she said and realised she wasn't. Not about going to this event with him anyway. It would give her a little time to prepare herself for what was going to happen later. And getting to know a bit more about the man she was planning to have her first and probably only wild fling with might not be a bad thing.

Added to that, she enjoyed social situations, meeting new people. And getting the chance to see Jace with his friends intrigued her. At school, he'd always been a loner despite the never-ending stream of girlfriends—unlike most of the other kids, he hadn't belonged to any specific clique, he'd never turned up for any after-school clubs or events and he hadn't participated in any of the sports teams. She suspected seeing how different he was now from that misfit boy would be another revelation.

'Whose party is it?' Assuming it was a party.

He lifted his hand off her leg, tucked one of the curls behind her ear as he hitched his shoulder in a lazy shrug. 'Just an associate. She's the reason I'm in London. And believe me, if she hadn't insisted on meeting up tonight, we wouldn't be here.' He leaned across the seat and kissed the side of her neck. Her pulse galloped against her skin. 'I can think of a few other things I'd much rather be doing,' he murmured. He took a deep breath in. 'You smell delicious.'

She.

Cassie's mind seized on the word as she struggled not to get sidetracked by the feel of his lips tracing across her collarbone. The man had seriously talented lips. 'Who is she?'

'Hmm?' he said nonchalantly, his hand moving to her waist.

'Are you involved with her?' She forced the question out, felt the shimmer of regret when his lips stopped nuzzling.

She couldn't see his expression clearly in the dim light of the car, her heart beating hard in her chest as she waited for a reply. She should have asked this question sooner. A lot sooner. She knew that she was young, free and single, as Nessa had put it. But she'd got so carried away with her own fantasies, she hadn't stopped to check if he was. She knew what kind of a guy he was where women were concerned. He hadn't exactly disguised it. She had no right to feel disappointed. But still the thought that he might be attached made her stomach turn over.

He touched her cheek, ran his thumb down to her chin. 'Exactly how much of a jerk do you think I am?'

The question sounded amused, but underneath she detected an edge. The breath she hadn't realised she was holding gushed out. She told herself the relief was purely physical. Having psyched herself up to enjoy tonight, it would be devastating to have the prize whisked away at the last minute.

'It's not that...' She wasn't judging him. She didn't have the right to judge him. This was just a one-night deal. For both of them. But even so, she would never allow herself to hurt another woman the way she'd been hurt. The way her mother had been hurt. 'It's just, I want to be sure you're not in a relationship. I wouldn't feel right sleeping with someone else's boyfriend.'

Jace stiffened at the question. He hated being asked about his personal life.

But this was his own stupid fault. He could hardly blame her for wanting to know more about him. He'd rushed things, indulged himself and this was the inevitable result.

He hadn't planned to get so carried away earlier. Had only planned to kiss her, but once he'd tasted her, she'd been so delicious, her response so artlessly seductive, he'd been consumed by the desire to taste more, like a starving man at a banquet, desperate to tuck in. The sound of her shocked little sighs as he'd stroked her thigh, the weight of her plump breasts pillowed against his chest, and the sultry Christmas scent of her hair had been so damned erotic he'd been rock hard in seconds. She'd been slick and wet and ready for him and the feel of her contracting around his fingers had nearly made him come in his pants. He'd had to use every last ounce of his control not to rip her clothes off and bury himself deep inside her. All thoughts of Helen's stupid party and the reasons why he'd flown three and a half thousand miles across the Atlantic had shot right out of his head. The desire to stay in the suite and spend the time devouring Cassie Fitzgerald instead had been all but irresistible. Which was exactly why he'd resisted it.

He should have won an Oscar for the performance he'd given, pretending he wasn't as affected as he looked. But he'd forced himself to hold back. Because he'd learned from experience that losing control and rushing into sex was never a good idea. He didn't do that any more and—once he'd managed to get his blood pressure back out of the danger zone— he'd remembered why.

Taking her to Helen's party for an hour had presented the perfect way to curb his lust without risking her running off. And seeing Helen again would bring him face to face with all the reasons why he couldn't afford to let his guard down with any woman—even one as apparently guileless as Cassie.

Given all of that, it shouldn't matter that she'd assumed the worst of him. He'd stopped caring about other people's opinions when he was a boy—when he'd figured out that it really made no difference what he did, they would always think the worst. But even Helen's constant and completely unfounded accusations of infidelity hadn't bothered him as much as the disappointment and resignation he could see in Cassie's wide blue eyes.

He didn't know Cassie and he didn't want to know her other than in a purely physical sense. The only connection they shared was a live-wire sexual chemistry that would soon burn out, once they'd both had their fill of each other. But even so, he couldn't quite deny the knot of tension in his shoulders.

'I'm not in a relationship,' he replied, struggling to keep his voice casual. 'And I wouldn't be trying to seduce you if I were.'

'I'm sorry,' she whispered. 'I didn't mean to imply...' she cleared her throat '...that you weren't honourable.'

The earnest statement was so sincere, he laughed, the tension dissolving as quickly as it had come. Settling his other hand on her waist, he dragged her closer. The movement tightened the seat belt under her breast and drew his gaze down to the enticing swell of her cleavage.

'Cassie, the one thing I've never been is honourable.' He pressed his face into her hair, let his lips linger on the fluttering pulse beneath her ear. 'If you had any idea how I plan to take advantage of you later tonight, you'd know exactly how dishonourable I am.'

She gave a husky little laugh that had his insides twisting into knots of a different kind. She tilted her head back; her bright gaze met his. 'I don't remember agreeing to come back with you tonight.'

'Yeah, but you will,' he said, his confidence returning full force as he saw her tongue dart out to wet her bottom lip. His palm rode down the curve of her hip, then snuck under her coat to caress the top of her thigh. 'How about I remind you how persuasive I can be?'

She grabbed his wrist, brought it firmly back to her waist. 'Let's not,' she said, her lips tilting in a nervous smile. 'We wouldn't want to shock the chauffeur.'

He lifted his hand to cup her cheek. 'Wouldn't we?'

She wiggled her eyebrows at him playfully. 'Not while he's driving.'

As if on cue, the screen slid down and the man in question spoke. 'We've arrived at the restaurant, Mr Ryan.'

'That was quick.' *Too damn quick.*

'Traffic was surprisingly light tonight, sir,' the driver replied.

Releasing the catch on Cassie's seat belt, Jace took her hand in his. 'Don't bother to get out, Dave,' he said through the partition.

Opening the car door, he stepped out, tugging Cassie out behind him.

'See you back here in an hour,' he said to the chauffeur as he closed the car door. An hour should be more than sufficient to calm himself down and make sure he was completely in control of this situation before he jumped Cassie again.

Cassie shivered as the car accelerated away. Sliding his palms under the opening of her coat, he placed a quick kiss on her forehead below her hairline. He wasn't risking going anywhere near her lips again until they had some privacy. 'Let's get this over with.'

Taking her hand firmly in his, he strode towards the entrance to the restaurant, impatience in every stride as he listened to the tap of her boot heels against the paving stones.

Taking a time-out to slow things down had been the smart thing to do, but right now, with a whole hour ahead of him before he could get her naked, he couldn't help wishing he'd been a lot more stupid.

Erotic anticipation rippled through Cassie's system as she stepped out into the lobby of the Tower's eighth floor. Her skin felt tight and itchy, and her pulse pounded against her throat like a metronome as Jace's masculine scent teased her nostrils, and his rough palm squeezed hers. Tonight would be an adventure that she intended to enjoy. For once she wasn't going to worry about tomorrow, she was going to concentrate on now.

Relax. Enjoy.

She repeated Nessa's mantra in her head. Then let out a staggered breath as Jace led her into a panoramic rooftop bar, its sleek lines and streamlined elegance reminding her of a vintage thirties ocean liner. Strobes of blue fluorescent light reflected off the forty-foot bar's steel panelling and illuminated a crowd dressed in everything from exclusive ball gowns and designer suits to artfully ripped denim. The loud buzz of conversation and the clink of glasses were only partially masked by the backing beat of drums and bass-guitar riffs coming from a live band at the far end of the room. Cassie's astonished gaze riveted on the wall of glass to her left, which framed a breathtaking view of the Thames' North Bank and the City of London beyond. The majesty of St Paul's Cathedral dome spotlit in the frosty twilight broke up the geometric shapes of the City's glaringly modern financial district.

Cassie hesitated, her fingers flexing in Jace's hand. 'Wow, no wonder this place is so popular.'

His grip tightened. 'Yeah,' he said, not sounding very impressed. 'Helen always knew how to throw a party.'

'Who's Helen?' she asked. But before she got a reply, Jace stiffened beside her. His jaw clenched as a tall woman in floating red silk made her way through the crowd towards them. The woman's figure was so thin and delicate, her collarbone stood out against the wispy straps of her gown. Either she was a supermodel or she had an eating disorder. Cassie opted for the former as she glided closer, deciding that her striking face, all high cheekbones, almond eyes and collagen-stung lips, could easily have graced the cover of a fashion magazine.

Dropping Cassie's hand, Jace placed his palm on her hip

to anchor her to his side. And she heard him swear under his breath.

'Hello, lover boy,' the woman said breathlessly as she drew level, her six-inch heels bringing her almost eye-level with Jace, and making Cassie feel like a midget. 'Long time, no see.' A cloud of expensive perfume engulfed Cassie as the woman leaned into him and pressed postbox-red lips to his. Her mouth lingered on his a moment too long for the kiss to be mistaken for platonic. Cassie wondered if she'd just become invisible.

Jace grasped the women's waist, deliberately setting her away from him. 'Where the hell is Bryan?' he asked, his tone frigid.

'That's for me to know and for you to find out,' she said, batting her eyelids as spots of colour appeared on her angular cheekbones.

'I didn't come all this way to play games, Helen,' he replied, his voice low with annoyance.

So this was Helen.

The woman's long eyelashes dipped in a bashful gesture that seemed out of keeping with the bold flirtation of a moment before and she gave a breathless little laugh. 'Don't be such a spoilsport.' She touched a perfectly manicured nail to Jace's chest. 'I have good news. I have some friends here tonight you must meet. I've whetted their appetite already and they're gagging to hear more about Artisan so they can invest.'

Catching her finger, Jace lowered it. 'You of all people know I'm not looking for new investment.'

She flicked her fingers in a dismissive gesture. 'Stop being difficult—you're not going to sell Artisan. I know how much the company means to you. I'm the one who watched you sweat blood over it.'

'It served its purpose,' he replied flatly. 'I don't get sentimental about business, any more than I get sentimental about the past.'

The chill in his voice sent a shiver of alarm up Cassie's spine. Who was this woman? And why did the familiarity between them remind her unpleasantly of the time when Lance had laughingly introduced her to his 'work colleague' Tracy at their New Year's Eve party last year?

She knew she didn't have any claim on Jace, this was just a casual date with the promise of wild sex for dessert, but that didn't make the uncomfortable feeling go away. She cleared her throat, loudly, and Helen's head whipped round.

The woman stared blankly at her as if she were noticing her for the first time, but made no move to introduce herself. Hostility rolled off her in waves, but there was something else there, a flicker of sadness and distress, that made Cassie wish she could disappear for real.

'Why don't I go get us a drink?' Cassie directed the question at Jace. Whatever was between these two, she was pretty sure she'd be better off not knowing what it was.

'We'll get one together,' he replied. 'I'll catch you later, Helen.'

But as he took Cassie's hand and went to sidestep their host she simply stepped the same way, blocking his path. 'What's the matter, Jace?' she said, her raised voice turning several heads by the bar. 'Does it make you uncomfortable introducing your little tart to your wife?'

He swore viciously as shock and disbelief made blood pound in Cassie's ears.

His wife?

Seeing the other guests staring at her, Cassie felt the blood pump into her cheeks. Jace said something, his voice low with temper, but she couldn't make out the words, the buzzing in her ears deafening her. Pulling her hand out of his, she rushed out of the bar and didn't look back.

She covered her mouth with her hand as reaction set in.

Oh, God, she was going to throw up.

So much for her fabulous adventure, she thought as she stabbed the lift button with frantic fingers. She should have seen it coming. Cassie Fitzgerald decided to have a wild fling and she ended up flinging herself straight into the arms of a married man. It would be ironic, if the guilt and embarrassment and the stupid sense of betrayal tumbling about in the pit of her stomach weren't making her gag.

'Hold up, Cassie.' A large hand wrapped around her forearm and whisked her round. 'Where the hell are you going?'

'Home.'

'Helen's not my wife,' he countered. 'We've been divorced for over five years now and separated a great deal longer. And up until about ten seconds ago I thought she'd be here with her new fiancé, so I didn't anticipate having to deal with this rubbish.'

The dispassionate explanation went some way to dispelling the nausea, but did nothing for the heat burning in her cheeks. 'Thanks for letting me know that,' she said, using sarcasm to mask the stupid sting of tears. What on earth was she so upset about? His relationship with his ex-wife really had nothing to do with her. 'It might have been nice if you'd told me a little sooner, though. Like when I asked about her in the car.'

'I'm not interested in talking about her or our marriage,' he said, as if withholding such a vital piece of information was perfectly reasonable.

'I specifically asked you if you were involved with her. And you didn't say a word.'

She stared at the lift display panel as if her life depended on it. She didn't want to look at him. And where the heck was the lift? It needed to get here before she did something really idiotic like bursting into tears. For some reason her emotions had been too close to the surface all night. Ever since she'd leapt into his car like a crazy lady—and then come apart on his sofa.

'Because there's nothing to say,' he huffed. 'I was never involved with her. Not in any real sense. Our marriage lasted exactly six months and I've regretted it ever since. The fact that she's delusional and insists on pretending there's still something between us is not my problem.' His thumb and forefinger gripped her chin and he directed her gaze back to his. 'Do you think you could look at me while you're having your snit?'

'This is not a snit.'

To her astonishment his lip curved up at one corner. 'It looks like one to me.'

'Excuse me, but you weren't the one who got called a little tart in front of three hundred people.'

The other corner curved up. 'I'm sure it was only two hundred and fifty,' he replied, his eyes now smiling too.

He placed a hand on her shoulder. She shrugged it off.

'Now, Cassie,' he said, amusement lightening his voice as he threaded his fingers into the fine hair at her nape. 'You're not looking on the bright side here.'

'What bright side?' she snapped, trying very hard not to be charmed by that sensual smile and the caressing touch. It wasn't fair. She'd been humiliated. Branded a tart by a woman she didn't even know. And he seemed to think it was a joke. She wasn't about to humour him.

Following her into the lift, he pressed the ground-floor button then placed his hands on either side of her head, caging her against the wall. 'The bright side is, we get to leave straight away. A whole hour earlier than planned.'

She braced her palms against his chest, but her arms felt heavy, sluggish, the coil of desire unravelling at an alarming speed and sapping her ability to push him away.

'You don't seriously think it's still game on for tonight, do you?' she said, trying for indignant but getting breathless instead.

He leaned down to suckle the pulse point in her neck. 'Uh-huh.'

'Well, you're wrong,' she sputtered, but her head dropped back, instinctively giving him better access.

His gaze, dark and intent, fixed on hers as he let one hand drop to snake under her coat and grip her waist. 'You're a terrible liar, you know.' He pulled her flush against him, all trace of amusement gone. 'Now tell me again you don't want me and I'll take you home.'

The gruff invitation and the feel of his rigid arousal pressing into her stomach made the words catch in her throat. She couldn't say it, because she did want him. And he was right, she'd never been a good liar.

She wanted him more than anything she'd ever wanted. Like a child in a sweet shop, offered the chance to grab as many delights as she could handle.

'It's not good to have everything you want,' she mumbled, mesmerised by the golden flecks that gilded the vivid green of his irises.

His thumb brushed across her nipple and she groaned, the aching tension that shot straight to her sex making resistance futile. 'It will be tonight,' he said.

The lift doors opened onto the ground-floor lobby and he eased back. Stepping out, he drew her with him, then dug into the back pocket of his jeans.

He flipped his phone open and dialled without taking his eyes off her. 'We're ready now, Dave. How soon can you get here?'

His lips tipped up as he listened to the reply. 'We'll be waiting.'

'How long is it going to take him?' she asked, her teeth

tugging on her lip. She might as well stop pretending that she wasn't going to jump him as soon as they got back to his suite. Because she wasn't fooling anyone, least of all herself.

It didn't matter that he hadn't told her about his ex-wife. It didn't even matter that the woman had called her a tart. All that mattered now was that the chemistry was hotter than molten lava—and she couldn't wait any longer to feel it erupt.

'Too damn long,' he said as the chauffeur-driven car squealed to a halt at the kerb.

CHAPTER SIX

'READY for your candy now?' Jace growled, his voice husky with lust and humour as he kicked the door of the suite shut.

Cassie giggled, adrenaline and desire coursing through her veins. Her back hit the lobby wall with a soft thud, the hard lines of his body flattening her breasts and making her belly throb.

'Yes, please,' she flirted back, sinking her fingers into the silky waves of his hair.

Don't think, just feel. And enjoy. Although relaxing was out of the question, seeing as she was about to explode.

They'd kissed and touched on the ride home, stoking the need to fever pitch, but through their clothes the caresses had been as frustrating as they were exciting.

He fastened his lips on her neck, his hands parting the flaps of her coat. The caress roamed over her hips, tugged up her tunic to settle on her behind. He dragged her towards him, grinding the hard bulge in his jeans against the swell of her stomach. 'You've got too many clothes on.'

Cassie ran her hands inside his leather jacket. Lifting the hem of his sweater, she finally touched bare skin. 'So do you,' she moaned.

Her fingertips explored the soft line of hair over washboard-lean abs, the warm skin like velvet over steel.

He shuddered, huffed out a laugh and stepped back. 'Let's remedy the situation.'

Shrugging off his jacket, he threw it on the floor. Then reached for her coat. She twisted to help him pull it off. Crossing his arms, he grasped his sweater and struggled out of it.

As he tossed the light jumper away Cassie stared, transfixed, at broad shoulders, beautifully defined pectoral muscles and the curls of dark hair that stood out in tufts under his arms, outlined flat brown nipples and then trailed down to bisect the ridges of his six pack and arrow beneath the buckle of his belt.

Her breath backed up in her lungs. That was one seriously gorgeous chest.

She watched him toe off one of his boots, then bend down to hop on one leg while yanking it off.

What was she doing? She should get naked too. She kicked off her own boots, then grasped the hem of her tunic just as his second boot hit the floor.

He grabbed her wrist, stopping her before she had raised the tunic past her midriff. 'No.'

She let go, the boldness fading. 'What's the matter?' Didn't he want her naked?

He swore softly, grunted the single word, 'Bedroom,' then started hauling her down the corridor.

He shoved open the door into a large, luxuriously furnished room with an enormous king-sized bed in the centre. Releasing her, he crossed to the bedside table, rummaged around for a second and then flung a cellophane-wrapped box onto the gold bedspread.

'Condoms,' he said unnecessarily. 'I figured I should locate them before I lost the ability to think.'

She smiled, ridiculously pleased to see he was as eager as she was. But when she went to take off her tunic again, he shot back across the room and took both her wrists in his, holding her hands manacled to her side.

'No. Wait.' He touched his forehead to hers, pressed his lips to her temple. 'There's no rush.' He breathed in her scent, eased out a steady breath. 'Let me do it.'

'Okay,' she said, surprised to feel an odd catch in her chest.

Taking the bottom of the tunic in his hands, he lifted it gently over her head, tossed it over his shoulder.

She sucked in a breath as the green of his eyes turned to a shining emerald. His dark gaze roamed over her, touching her skin like a physical caress, burning a trail of fire from her cheeks, to her breasts, blazing into her sex and sizzling right down to her toes.

He slid his thumbs and forefingers under the straps of her simple cotton bra, then tugged them off her shoulders. Her breasts became heavy, the nipples swelling into hard peaks as he peeled the cups down, exposing her to his gaze.

The dark arousal flared. 'Damn,' he murmured. 'You're perfect.'

The little catch in her chest clutched at her heart. No one had ever thought she was perfect before. Let alone said so.

Reaching around her waist, he drew her closer. His lips buzzed her shoulder where the strap had left a red mark as he released the catch on her bra. He dragged it free, flung that away too.

His eyes met hers as he cradled the weight in his palms, circled her nipples with his thumbs. Then he bent to fasten his lips on one aching peak.

Cassie threaded her fingers into the hair at the side of his head, and arched into his mouth, the hot, wet suction sending her senses into overdrive. He suckled strongly, drawing her into his mouth, then pulling back to flick his tongue over the tip, massaging and teasing her other breast with his fingers.

A sob escaped as she writhed. It wasn't just his fingers

that were talented, it seemed. She'd never realised she was so sensitive there. The raw nerves pulsated as moisture flooded between her thighs.

The pressure built and intensified at her core as sparks of fire originated in her nipples, fanned out across her breasts, then darted down to her centre. She shut her eyes, her legs like wet noodles as he transferred his mouth to her other breast.

He stopped the devastating caresses briefly to tear off her tights and panties, then as his mouth returned to her pounding breasts he flattened his palm against her stomach, pressed the heel of his hand onto her aching centre, then delved into the curls at the apex of her thighs.

He circled for several agonising seconds, then flicked his finger over the heart of her. She cried out, bucked against his palm, the sparks triggering an explosion of need that reared up and crashed through her as he continued to rub the swollen nub. She dug her nails into his shoulders, braced herself as her legs gave out and the final waves of pleasure drained her body, leaving her as limp as a rag doll.

He gave a strained laugh, and bent down to lift her onto his shoulder. 'Come on, Cassidy,' he said, his hand patting her bare buttocks. 'Time for bed.'

Her stomach rode the ridge of his shoulder blade as he strode across the room and dropped her on the mattress. She watched in a daze as he kicked off his jeans and boxers and climbed onto the bed.

Shock reverberated through her, widening her eyes and slicing through the haze of afterglow, as she stared at the massive erection that prodded her thigh when he settled beside her.

As if in a dream, she reached out and touched her nail to the tip. It bobbed towards her, as if it had a life of its own.

'You're perfect too,' she whispered. A strange combination of euphoria and excitement tightened like a vice around her heart. And for the first time ever she let instinct take over, the heady endorphins of her recent climax making her yearn to give him the same pleasure he had given her.

She trailed her finger down the line of hair on his belly, then wrapped her hand around the solid length of his erection. It felt hard and smooth against her palm. But it wasn't enough, not nearly enough. She pushed at his shoulders until he lay on his back. He thrust his fingers into her hair, as she ran a trail of kisses across his magnificent chest.

His fingers flexed, massaging her scalp, as she inched lower, sliding her tongue over his six pack, licking at the ridge of his belly button, then delving within. The muscles of his flat belly tensed as she encountered the powerful erection at last. Darting her tongue out, she licked up the length of him like an ice lolly, then took the swollen head between her lips.

He swore, shuddered, then, cradling her cheeks in his palms, yanked her off him as he jerked into a sitting position.

Colour flooded into her cheeks as she scrambled back onto her knees. She'd done it wrong. 'Sorry, you don't like that?' she said, the euphoria fading as inadequacy flooded in.

Lance had always told her what to do, had hated it when she took the lead. Why was she so rubbish at sex?

He gave a strained laugh, then reached for her. 'Are you kidding? I love it,' he said, sliding his palm over her shoulder to pull her closer. 'But we'll have to save it for later or I'm not going to last long enough to get inside you.'

'Oh, I see,' she said, feeling gauche and yet ridiculously relieved. She hadn't done it wrong after all.

Shifting over, he reached for the condoms. Tearing the cellophane, he dumped the contents out on the bedspread. He grabbed one of the packages and fumbled with it. 'Someone ought to tell the manufacturers they use too much packaging,' he grumbled, finally ripping it with his teeth.

As he flipped out the rubber she took his wrist. 'Do you

mind if I do it?' she asked, the urge to touch him again overwhelming.

'Do I mind?' His eyebrow rose a fraction. 'Of course not.'
He smiled and passed it to her. 'Be my guest.'

Lying back on the bedspread, he crossed his arms behind
his head, and watched her with heavy-lidded eyes, the desire
in them so palpable her heart pounded against her ribcage.

Holding the slick contraceptive in her fingers as if she were
handling nitroglycerine, she gave a faltering sigh, anticipation
and trepidation colliding to make her heart beat double time.
Her eyes feasted on the beauty of his body, wisps of dark hair
highlighting the masculine planes of sleek muscles and lean
sinews. Then her heart throbbed right into her throat as she
focused on the magnificent evidence of how much he wanted
her. He was all hers for tonight, and she didn't want to muck
it up. She didn't want this to be going-through-the-motions
sex, or, worse, bad sex. Just this once she wanted what Nessa
had promised her. She wanted really amazing sex.

'Cassidy, I hate to rush you,' he said, jerking her out of
her stupor. 'But if you keep looking at me like that, I'm not
going to be responsible for my actions.'

The sensual threat made her smile.

Do not overthink this.

She rolled the lubricated latex down the thick length with
careful fingers, confidence surging through her as he sucked
in a shaky breath and the muscles of his abdomen quivered.

Taking her by the shoulders, he swivelled round, so that
she would be lying beneath him. But she reared up. 'Could I
be on top?'

He gave a tense laugh. 'Absolutely,' he said, then framed
her face with his hands. 'I'm always happy to oblige a woman
who knows what she wants.'

He rolled to reverse their positions, then skimmed his
hands down to cradle her bottom as she kneeled over him,

lifting her above the enormous erection. 'Climb aboard, candy girl.'

She laughed, the compliment burning away the last of her inhibitions in a rush of pure unadulterated pleasure. Directing the powerful shaft to her entrance, she lowered herself onto him.

He was big, bigger than she had expected, and her bottom lip caught on her teeth as she tightened around him. She tried to force her hips down, but the pleasure dimmed, the penetration too full, the stretched feeling unbearable.

'I can't do it.'

'Shh, relax,' he crooned. 'Take it slowly. You're tensing up.' He lifted her, sat up, deftly adjusting their positions so that his lips could fasten on her breasts while seeking fingers touched her core. The hot suction of his mouth, the clever caresses had pleasure returning in a rush. She sobbed as she began to move, her hips undulating to relieve the pressure, then sinking down farther to let it build again. Instinctive, basic, she gloried in the ability to control the penetration, throwing her head back, and clasping his shoulders.

'That's it, Cassie.' He lifted his head from her breast, his fingers continuing to circle her clitoris as his other arm banded around her bottom, urging her into a devastating rhythm. 'You've got it, sweetheart. Once more. You're almost there.'

She plunged down, the encouragement spurring her on, and took him in to the hilt at last.

The huge erection bumped her cervix and touched a place deep inside, the waves of pleasure quickly swelling into an uncontrollable torrent.

His ragged breathing rasped in her ears as she rode him frantically, driving them both to completion. The contractions held her body in a vicelike grip for what seemed like an eternity and she cried out, revelling in the sheer joy of the wild ride. He shouted out his release as she tumbled into the abyss, shattering into a billion quivering shards of light.

She fell forward, knocking him back, their sweat-slicked bodies collapsing onto the bed.

He hugged her, holding her on top, his deep, satisfied laugh brushing against her ear lobe. 'Cassie, that was…' he paused, his hands stroking her back, the still-huge erection pulsing inside her '…amazing.'

Her heart flipped over, afterglow turning into the sweet glow of triumph. 'No, it wasn't,' she said, a wonderfully smug smile curving her lips. 'It was *really* amazing.'

He brushed her hair back from her face, the confidential smile on his lips reminding her of the secret joke they had once shared on a stairwell. 'Yeah, really amazing,' he said, and her heart soared.

CHAPTER SEVEN

'WAKE up, sweet cheeks. Dinner's here.'

Cassie's eyes fluttered open to find Jace sitting on the edge of the bed, gently stroking her cheek with the palm of his hand. He wore one of the hotel's monogrammed robes, but the wisps of chest hair revealed in the V of pristine white towelling had sensation shimmering across her skin. Heat rode up her neck as she felt the unfamiliar tenderness between her thighs—and the recollection of what he'd done to her, of what they'd done to each other, came flooding back.

'I fell asleep?' she asked, her voice groggy and confused. All she could remember was lying curled in his arms, feeling sated and better about herself than she had felt in a long time, her bottom butting his softening erection and his hands resting on her belly.

'We both did,' he said, his thumb running down her neck and over her collarbone, then slipping beneath the edge of the fine linen sheet to touch the tender skin of her breasts. 'Really amazing sex will do that to a person.'

She stretched, stifling a yawn, and luxuriated in the feeling of triumph.

It *had* been really amazing. Hadn't it?

But then her nostrils caught the sent of tarragon and roast meat and her stomach grumbled audibly, making the flush spread.

He chuckled. 'Unfortunately, really amazing sex also makes you ravenous.'

She lifted up on her elbows as he stood and walked across the room.

'I ordered us some fancy French chicken dish to keep our strength up,' he said as he lifted another monogrammed robe off an armchair.

A quick grin lifted her lips. He wanted her to keep her strength up. That sounded promising.

He returned with the fluffy white robe, held it up for her. 'But you have to put this on first, or I'm liable to start ravishing you instead of the food.'

She pushed back the sheet, and made herself hop out of bed, concentrating on her hunger to stave off the silly spurt of shyness about her nakedness. Which was patently ridiculous given what they'd been doing before she drifted off.

'What time is it?' she asked, shoving her hands into the sleeves.

He wrapped the robe around her, tying the belt from behind and then hugged her round the waist. His nose nudged the top of her head. 'Nearly eleven.'

She'd been asleep for *three* hours!

She pulled out of his embrace, swung round, dismayed and desperately disappointed.

Would he expect her to go home? She had no idea what the etiquette for one-night stands was, but she had a feeling staying until the morning might be awkward.

He frowned. 'Damn, you're a vegetarian, right?'

'No, I...'

He took her chin, his brow creasing. 'Then what's the matter?'

She swallowed. She might as well ask. She had a right to ask. 'What are we going to do *after* dinner?'

'*After* dinner,' he said, his lips quirking. 'Well, now.'

Gripping her hips, he tugged her easily towards him. 'After dinner, I figured we could try out the whirlpool tub in the master bathroom. Considering the rates this place charges, I haven't made nearly enough use of it. And then—' he wiggled his eyebrows comically '—I thought lots more really amazing sex wouldn't go amiss.' The teasing expression sobered a little. 'If you're not too sore, that is,' he added. 'You weren't kidding when you said it had been a while for you, were you?'

The thrill of arousal rushed through her, tempered by the little clutch in her chest at the concern in his eyes. She'd always thought of him as being dangerous. And he was. Even more so now she knew how devasting he was in bed. But how could she have guessed that he would also be such a considerate lover?

'I'm not sore,' she said, deciding to ignore his probing question. She certainly didn't intend to tell him how long it had been. Or why.

She placed her palms on his bare chest, felt the thunder of his heartbeat matching hers. 'But you may still have to persuade me,' she teased, twirling one of her fingers in his chest hair, the fine art of flirtation and temptation coming as naturally as breathing.

He laughed, taking her finger and bringing it to his lips. 'Don't worry, I intend to.' He gave it a nip, then groaned as his stomach growled loudly. 'But first we better eat. We're likely to need it. For stamina.'

She let all the deliciously dangerous thoughts of what the night ahead might hold drown out any doubts as he led her into the suite's living room. But her steps faltered, her bare feet sinking into the silk rug, when she saw the ornate table laid with gilt-edged china plates covered with silver domes, a bottle of champagne chilling in an ice-bucket and a single tapered candle illuminating the table with the help of the fire glowing in the open hearth. Her heartbeat slowed at the romantic scene, but she quashed the sentiment as he held out her chair for her.

She propped her elbows on the table and forced herself not to overthink things as she admired his darkly handsome face in the flickering light.

He was only hers for one night. That was all she wanted. One night of really amazing sex, which she wasn't going to ruin—as she had so many times before—with misguided hopes of romance.

'Voilà!' He whisked the dome covering her plate with a flourish. 'Tuck in.'

Taking a sighing breath of the delicious scent rising from the plate, she lifted the heavy silver knife and fork, intending to do just that.

Jace watched Cassie lick the creamy tarragon sauce off her lower lip and felt the now familiar heat pulse in his groin. Diverting his attention to his own plate, he sliced into the succulent chicken breast, let the rich aroma of butter and herbs go some way to dispelling the spicy scent of her that seemed to have invaded his senses.

Problem was, he wasn't just hungry for food. He took a swallow of the delicious dish. And controlling his appetite for Cassie Fitzgerald was proving to be more of a challenge than he had anticipated.

After waking up with her curled in his arms, he'd lain awake for twenty minutes. Torturing himself with the feel of her plump breasts rising and falling against his forearm, her soft buttocks pillowed against his reinvigorated erection, and recalled their lovemaking in every exquisite, excruciating detail.

He pictured her gorgeous breasts after he'd taken off her bra. The large, rosy nipples rigid with arousal as he teased the swollen tips with his teeth. Then her pale cheeks flushed with colour, her lips slightly parted, the harsh sobs of her orgasm as his fingers sank into the wet heat at her core. Her limp body draped over his shoulder. And at last, the incredible feel of her full lips caressing his erect flesh.

He'd never seen a more erotic sight, and had been forced to stop her before he went off like a rocket. But he'd instantly regretted it when she'd lurched away, the desire and excitement in her eyes snuffed out by regret and panic.

He'd never met a woman who was so effortlessly seductive, who could turn him inside out with lust without doing much more than breathing and yet was so unsure of herself.

Some guy had clearly done a number on her. That could be the only answer. And as he'd listened to her sleep and resisted the urge to wake her up and ravish her all over again, he'd felt his curiosity—and his anger—grow.

He'd struggled to get a grip on both before he did something idiotic. So he'd eased her out of his arms, and climbed out of bed to arrange dinner.

While he'd run a bath in the enormous whirlpool tub, then sat in the lounge waiting for their meal to arrive, he'd contemplated exactly how he was going to play things for the rest of the night, and had come to a few important conclusions.

Cassie Fitzgerald was sweet and sexy and just what he needed after his dry spell. He'd spent far too many months recently sweating over the direction of his business and more specifically figuring out the best way to cut the last of his ties to his ex-wife—and his sex life had suffered as a result.

Maybe he wasn't anywhere near as prolific as he had been in his teens, but he wasn't a man who dealt all that well with months of abstinence. His explosive, uncontrolled reaction to Cassie in the first place was evidence of that.

That Cassie was the complete antithesis of the women he usually chose to date, who were as jaded as he was in the

sack, was the only reason why he found her so captivating—
and so refreshing. But making an issue of it by satisfying his
curiosity about her past wasn't an option. It had been quite
a while since he'd had a one-night stand, but he knew that
mixing sex with intimacy was always a mistake.

This trip was about correcting the mistakes of his past, his
marriage being the biggest one of all; getting involved with
anyone would kind of defeat the purpose of the whole enter-
prise.

He planned to enjoy this evening, and he wanted Cassie to
enjoy it too. From her fragile confidence and her touchingly
insecure reactions when they made love, he suspected she
hadn't got to enjoy sex nearly as much as she should have in
the past. And maybe it was arrogant of him, but while he'd
never professed to know what women wanted emotionally—
and didn't intend to find out—he'd made it his life's work to
know what they enjoyed in bed.

Cassie's sexual liberation was a little project that he was
more than happy to dedicate himself to. Especially as Cassie
seemed so receptive to the idea. Anything else wasn't going to
happen. So he wasn't about to risk encouraging her to think
this was more by asking her personal questions.

But as he took a pensive sip of his champagne and Cassie's
eyes met his he noticed the potent mix of desire and reticence
in their depths and couldn't quite ignore the thorn digging
into his side.

Setting his glass down, he reached across the table and anchored the errant curl of hair that had fallen across Cassie's
cheek back behind her ear.

'How's the food?' he asked.

'Delicious,' she said, and his gut tightened right up again.

He'd always had a bad habit, he thought wryly, of finding
the forbidden irresistible. That was why he'd spent a night
redecorating the school gym at seventeen and ended up get-

ting arrested. And it was also why he'd been unable to resist sleeping with his main investor's daughter years later, and got trapped in a marriage of convenience that had caused him no end of headaches. He thought he'd learned to curb the impulse to do something he knew he would later regret.

But as Cassie's gaze flicked back to her plate the dangerous impulse took charge of his tongue and he heard himself saying, 'Correct me if I'm wrong, Cassidy, but I got the impression earlier that you're not a veteran of really amazing sex?'

Cassie jerked her chin up, stunned by the perceptive question. And what it might mean. Why had he asked that? And how did he know? Was her lack of proficiency that obvious?

She pushed out a laugh. 'Why would you think that?' she scoffed, deciding to bluff. Unfortunately, the colour charging into her cheeks wasn't exactly playing along.

He pushed his plate aside, the quizzical smile he sent her making the colour charge faster. 'There's no need to be embarrassed,' he said, not just calling her bluff, but trampling all over it. 'I'm surprised, that's all.' Placing his hands behind his head, he stretched back as he studied her, making the chair creak and the robe fall open revealing a tantalising glimpse of those mouth-watering abdominal muscles.

She reached for her champagne flute, trying not to follow the line of hair bisecting his abs, which she now knew arrowed down to something even more enticing.

'You're a beautiful woman, with an extremely passionate nature,' he said, his voice so low she was sure she could feel it reverberating across some of the tender places he'd explored so thoroughly earlier in the evening. 'I just wondered why you haven't indulged it more?'

She gulped and put the glass down, grateful that she hadn't taken a sip of the champagne yet.

An extremely passionate nature! Had he actually said that? About her?

She was both stunned and flattered by his assessment, and her heart squeezed a little. It had never been her fault that first David then Lance couldn't remain faithful, and now she had indisputable proof. Jace Ryan, who was a much more talented man than either of them would ever be, found her beautiful and extremely passionate.

She felt both vindicated and empowered by the thought, and her recently activated flirt gene flickered back to life. 'Because, of course, you'd be an expert on that,' she teased, determined to steer the conversation away from anything too personal. She certainly didn't plan to talk about her past relationships with men, because that would ruin the nice little buzz from his compliment.

One dark brow lifted. 'An expert on what?'

'Indulging an extremely passionate nature.'

He huffed out a laugh. 'Guilty as charged.' Tilting his chair forward, he stood up. Taking her hands in his, he tugged her out of the chair. 'But I definitely think your extremely passionate nature needs a lot more indulgence. And tonight I'm more than happy to sacrifice myself for the cause.'

Her pulse points pounded.

How easy would it have been for her to start tumbling into love with a man as overpowering as Jace Ryan last Christmas, with a lot less encouragement than really amazing sex and a few casual compliments? But luckily now she was much more pragmatic. He didn't know anything about her or her past, so he couldn't possibly know how much this night meant to her.

And she had no intention of letting him find out.

'That's very noble of you,' she whispered cheekily, glad to have deflected his questioning so easily.

He gave the tie on her robe a slow tug, until it released, the flaps falling open. His rough palms brushed around her waist and cupped her bare bottom. 'I thought so,' he said, a mischievous gleam in his eyes as moisture flooded between her thighs.

He pushed the robe off her shoulders and she gave a soft gasp as it dropped to the floor. Then yelped as he lifted her into his arms.

'Time for your next lesson,' he said as he carried her into the bathroom. 'Really amazing sex in a whirlpool tub.'

She clasped her arms round his neck and clung on, laughing while her senses stampeded into overdrive—the tight squeeze in her heart drowned out by the frantic beat of arousal and the loud splash as he dumped her into warm scented water.

CHAPTER EIGHT

'I'M GOING to be stuck in London on business until New Year's Day,' Jace's voice murmured in Cassie's ear, his soap-slicked hands cupping her heavy breasts and lazily teasing the nipples with his thumbs. 'Have you got any plans for the Christmas period?'

A little shocked by the renewed jolt of heat, and a lot more shocked by the casual enquiry, Cassie shifted in his lap, feeling the heavy arousal nestled between her legs, and her heart leapt into her throat.

After they'd soaped each other into a frenzy, he'd insisted she sit on the edge of the huge tub so he could take her into his mouth. She'd never felt anything so exquisite in her life before, the rough, expert play of his tongue on her sensitised clitoris quickly becoming more than she could bear. But when she'd come down from the intense high, the look of satisfaction on his face had made her feel ever so slightly vulnerable.

She was feeling a lot more vulnerable now.

'Why do you ask?' And why had her heart just rocketed into her throat at his question? He couldn't be suggesting what she thought he was suggesting? Could he? That they should extend their one-night fling?

He rubbed his palms over the rigid peaks and chuckled when a moan slipped out. 'Because I want more time to play with you while I'm here. One night isn't going to be enough.'

There it was again, the smug tone of voice—and the bump of her heart in her throat.

'The water's getting cold,' she said, levering herself out of his lap.

But before she could climb out, his large hands bracketed her hips, holding her in place. 'Why didn't you answer my question?' he said as she glanced over her shoulder.

He didn't look hurt or offended. Why would he? But even so she couldn't quite bring herself to give him a straight answer. The desire to say yes to his suggestion was so powerful, she knew it had to be a bad idea.

She wasn't the naive little twit she'd been for the first twenty-seven years of her life. She'd turned a corner in the last ten months and she would never go back to that. Believing all the empty promises her father had told her as a child, only to be left devastated when he never lived up to any of them. Or falling for David at art college, only to be told she wasn't what he was looking for. Or, worst of all, accepting a proposal from a man who, during the whole three years he'd bunked at her flat while he was 'between jobs', she now suspected had never been faithful to her.

But while she knew she had finally learned her lesson with Lance—that men were about as reliable as the electrical appliances you bought from a door-to-door salesman—she wasn't at all happy about the way her heart was leaping about in her chest. Just as it had done all those years ago when her father had rung up from Tokyo or Rome or San Francisco to tell her he'd definitely see her that weekend... Or when Lance had got down on one knee on the tiny balcony of her flat on Valentine's Day and asked her to marry him...

She wasn't a sucker any more, but was she completely cured? And did she really want to put her new, cynical self to the test with a man like Jace? Especially at Christmas time, when losing your grip on reality was practically a requirement of the season?

Crossing her arms over her bare breasts, she wriggled out of his grip and stepped out of the tub.

'Hey, come back here. You haven't given me an answer,' he said.

Grabbing a large fluffy white towel from the neatly folded pile on the vanity, she wrapped it round her dripping body.

'Why don't we talk about it later?' she offered. 'I'm not sure what I'm doing over the next week or so,' she added, glad she sounded so blasé when she didn't feel blasé. She secured the towel over her breasts and glanced back, fluttering her eyelashes for all she was worth. 'And I thought you promised me more really amazing sex?' she said, deciding that flirtation was the best defence.

She heard the splash as he followed her out of the tub. And gulped as she watched him in the mirror, her eyes devouring the sight of his naked body, glistening wet. His arm reached over her to grab another towel.

'Are you trying to distract me?' he murmured against her hair as she watched his reflection hook the towel around his waist.

'Is it working?' she asked, tilting her head to see the hot look on his face.

His hands circled her waist, tugged her back against his chest. 'What do you think?'

Arousal charged through her system as the feel of something hard and insistent butted against her bottom through the layers of towelling. 'Yes,' she murmured.

Turning her in his arms, he gripped the top of her towel in his fist. 'You know, you're a much badder girl than I gave you credit for.'

'Bad is more fun, remember,' she quipped back. 'You said so yourself.'

'So I did.' He pressed his lips to hers, distracting her, while he loosened her towel with a quick tug. 'But from now on there are rules.'

'Rules?' She grasped the fist he had on her towel with both hands as the knot slipped. 'What rules?'

'For starters—' he manacled her wrists in one hand, lifted her fingers to his lips, forcing her to let go of his fist, then whipped her towel off with the other '—I want you naked.'

'Oh,' she said, the blush spreading up her neck at the wicked grin on his face as her towel dropped to her feet. 'Well, fine,' she said, wrestling her hands free from his grasp. 'But I happen to believe in women's rights.' She slid her hands under his towel and yanked it free. 'Which means the same goes for you.'

He laughed, not remotely embarrassed by the powerful erection standing up against his belly. 'Good thing I happen to be a firm believer in women's rights,' he said playfully, then grabbed her and hoisted her onto his shoulder. She shrieked, kicked, giggled, but didn't struggle too hard, distracted somewhat by the upsidedown view of a very nice male behind.

'Or you'd be in serious trouble now,' he finished as he marched her into the bedroom. Tossing her onto the bed, he climbed up after her, the wicked gleam in his eye so full of purpose she wondered if she ought to make a run for it.

His hand gripped her ankle and he dragged her beneath him before she could make up her mind. 'But I'm still going to want an answer.' Cupping her hips, he cradled the thick erection against her belly. 'Eventually.'

'I'll give you an answer later.' She ran her hands over his broad shoulders, let her fingers caress the strong column of his neck and fist in the hair at his nape as he sheathed himself efficiently with the condom.

Much later.

She couldn't think about his suggestion now, couldn't let it ruin the rush of excitement tingling along her skin.

He grasped her hips, and she lifted up, taking his mouth in a seeking kiss. He eased into her as his tongue thrust, the penetration so deep it took her breath away. Pleasure blindsided her as he rocked in short, sharp, devastating thrusts. She built to peak with startling speed, the fanciful leap of her heartbeat, the questions racing in her head, lost in the roar of ecstasy.

'About the next week or so.' Jace brushed the flat of his hand over the curve of her bottom, struggling to focus his mind and sound nonchalant while his body was still humming. 'What's your answer?'

'Hmm?' Her soft breasts snuggled against his side as her nose pressed into his neck and her hand rested against his chest.

He hoped to hell she couldn't feel the way his heart was battering his ribs.

'I want to do more of this.' He turned his head, placed a kiss on her forehead. 'How about you?' he finished, a little surprised he was having to press the point.

Why hadn't she already leapt at the chance to have an affair with him?

Suggesting it had seemed like little more than a formality in the bath, given the way she'd responded to him so far. Damn it, she'd nearly passed out when he'd put his mouth on her—and watching her come apart like that had been exquisitely arousing. But instead of agreeing to the suggestion, she'd been instantly evasive, just like when he'd asked her about her past over dinner. And he'd had to face the unthinkable prospect that she might say no.

He wasn't so arrogant as to believe every woman wanted to jump into bed with him, but the sexual chemistry between them was explosive. Any fool could see that. She wanted him all right. She wanted him a lot. So why had she refused to give him a straight answer? Was there some problem he wasn't seeing? And why had the thought that there was a problem piqued his curiosity about her even more? Usually if a woman put up any resistance he backed off instantly. But with her he couldn't seem to let it go.

It had been a long time since he'd been stupid enough to let his sex drive dictate his actions. But even knowing he should probably back off, he knew he wasn't going to.

He had close to two weeks in London to meet a series of European buyers and deal with his ex-wife's solicitors—so he could sell Artisan and finally shove the skeletons of his past back in the closet they had lurched out of and forget about them for good.

For a man who had spent the last fourteen years of his life working eighteen- to twenty-hour days—and playing pretty hard in the hours that were left—the next thirteen days spread out before him like a long, slow canter into extreme boredom. The fact that it was Christmas wasn't a big help either.

He wasn't a fan of the festive season. All that false bon-homie and conspicuous consumption got on his nerves—and having to endure it in the place he'd struggled so hard to get out of was going to add a nice thick layer of irritability to his aversion. Sure, the five-star luxury of The Chesterton was a far cry from the cramped council flat in Shepherd's Bush where he'd grown up—which was the main reason he'd booked the best suite here, the difference proving to him just how far he'd come from that unhappy troublesome kid—but he'd left this city for a reason, and being forced back here by Helen and her recent interference in the company hadn't improved his disposition one bit.

Until Cassie had leapt into his car with an indignant scowl

on her cute face and those deliciously full breasts spilling out of her drenched coat.

He gripped her waist and jostled her slightly. 'So, Cassidy, what's it to be?' he murmured into her hair, her enticing cinnamon scent made even more tempting mixed with the fresh scent of the hotel's vanilla soap. He imagined all the fun they could have together as he waited for her to reply, ready to do some serious persuasion if she didn't give him the answer he wanted.

The next two weeks would be the opposite of boring with Cassie in his bed. So he wasn't about to let her give him some lame excuse. A grin split his features, and luckily she happened to be uniquely susceptible to his powers of persuasion.

Having taken a moment to mull that satisfying fact over in his head, he tilted his chin down to peer into her face. And the smug smile vanished.

Her eyelashes touched the flushed skin of her cheeks while the steady murmur of her breathing brushed against his collarbone.

He cursed under his breath. *Unreal.* She'd only gone and fallen fast asleep on him.

CHAPTER NINE

SEDUCTIVE, intensely erotic images swirled in Cassie's head as she drifted out of a dream-filled sleep. Her eyelids fluttered open and the fierce tug of arousal pulsing in her sex intensified as she became aware of the muscular forearm banded under her breasts. Deep, even breathing brushed the top of her head and a warm body pressed against her back.

Jace.

She blinked at the thin winter sunlight gilding the opulent furnishings of his hotel suite and shifted slightly, the tenderness between her thighs so acute it was almost as if he were still lodged inside her. A hot flush swept through her as the erotic images from her dream recurred in vivid detail. And she realised they weren't dreams at all, but memories.

She tensed as Jace's sleep-roughened murmur made the hair on the back of her neck prickle. His arm tightened briefly under her breasts and then relaxed back into sleep.

Waiting a minute to make sure he was completely asleep, she took a moment to enjoy the feel of being wrapped so securely in his embrace.

A wistful smile curled her lips. So Jace Ryan was a snuggler? Who would have thought it?

Dispelling the thought and the tightening in her chest that accompanied it, she scooted over in incremental movements, then gingerly lifted his arm from around her waist and placed it behind her.

He grunted, and she sucked in a breath, praying he wouldn't wake up.

Then he flopped over onto his back, taking the sheet with him, and she let out the breath she'd been holding. She twisted round, then hesitated, momentarily mesmerised by the handsome face thrown into sharp relief by the morning sunlight peeking through the room's heavy velvet curtains. With his jaw shadowed by morning stubble, the thick locks of hair falling across his brow and that magnificent body bare right down to the springy curls of hair that peeked above the sheet draped low on his hips, it took Cassie a moment to catch her breath.

He had to be the most beautiful man she'd ever seen. And he'd been all hers for the wildest night of her life. She forced herself to look away and climb off the bed as carefully as possible so as not to wake him.

The night was over now and she needed to go home. He'd asked her about extending their fling, and as much as she yearned to wake him up and accept the offer she wasn't going to. She couldn't take the risk. While she might want to believe she could be smart and sensible about a brief fling with Jace and just concentrate on enjoying lots of really amazing sex for the next week or so, she didn't entirely trust herself. Those silly clutches in her heartbeat, last night and this morning, were proof that her delusional tendencies hadn't quite died the death she'd hoped in the last nine months... And she wasn't ready yet to tempt fate with someone as devastating as Jace Ryan.

It was cowardly and fairly pathetic, but she could live with that. What she couldn't live with was the thought of making a fool of herself all over again with yet another man who had

nothing to offer her. Her brow creased as the pulse of awareness rippled across her nerve endings.

Well, apart from lots of really amazing sex, that is.

She gathered up her tunic and underwear from the other
side of the room, determined not to give in to the tempting
thought. But she couldn't quite resist returning to the bedside
to study him while he slept as she slipped on her clothing.

As she sat in the chair by the bed, and rolled on the luxury
silk tights he'd bought her, it occurred to her that, unlike the
other men she'd known, Jace didn't look any more vulnerable in sleep than he did when he was awake.

Was that part of his allure? she wondered. Was that the
quality that had made him so irresistible last night but made
her so wary of him in the cold light of morning? That, unlike
her, he seemed so sure of himself? So controlled? Even in the
throes of lovemaking, at the height of passion, he hadn't lost
the commanding, almost ruthless self-confidence of someone who knew exactly what he wanted out of life. And was
more than prepared to do whatever he had to do to get it.

Standing up, she smoothed damp palms down the beaded
tunic, then leant over the bed and pressed the lightest of kisses
to the rough stubble on his cheek. The tantalising musk of
vanilla soap and man filled her senses.

'Goodbye, Jace,' she whispered.

Then she turned and hurried from the room, trying exceptionally hard not to think about missing out on the sexiest,
most exhilarating Christmas of her entire life. Or the painful
ache under her breastbone that she refused to interpret.

She'd done the smart, sensible thing. She was now offi-
cially a grown-up.

Cassie's ink pen jolted as the doorbell buzzed, sending a thick
black line slashing through the Sugar Plum Fairy's nose and
ruining two hours' work.

She cursed and dropped the pen into the cup she kept at the side of her drawing easel. It was her own stupid fault. She shouldn't have attempted to design her Christmas cards today. She'd been jumpy ever since she'd got back from the West End, her hormones refusing to settle down despite all her best efforts.

The doorbell buzzed again. Wiping her hands with a washcloth, she got up and walked from her bedroom, through the tiny living room to the front door, ruthlessly quashing the hope that it might be Jace. He didn't even know where she lived. And anyway, she didn't want to see him; the endorphin withdrawal he'd caused was quite hard enough to deal with without the added stimulation of seeing him again.

Unlocking the deadbolt, she pulled the door open.

'Hey there, what's up?' Nessa grinned, holding up a grease-spotted bag from the bakery downstairs. 'I brought apple Danish to bribe you into talking about your new man over morning coffee.' She breezed past Cassie into the flat, her extensions arranged in corkscrew curls that bobbed around her shoulders as she waltzed into the kitchen.

Cassie stifled a groan. She loved Nessa like a sister. But the last thing she needed right now was to have to relive her wild night with Jace.

'He's not my new man,' she grumbled. Or not any more. She followed Nessa into the snug galley kitchen. 'And anyway it's nearly lunchtime,' she moaned, attempting to redirect the conversation. 'Pastries will spoil our appetite.' Not to mention apply several extra pounds to her hips, which she probably didn't need. A vision of Jace's ex-wife with her skeletal supermodel figure popped into Cassie's head.

Correction, which she *definitely* didn't need.

Bending to grab Cassie's coffee jar out of the fridge, Nessa gave a rich chuckle. 'You're very grumpy this morning.' She straightened, shooting Cassie a knowing smile and not looking redirected in the least. 'Couldn't be because you didn't get enough sleep last night?' She wiggled her eyebrows before ladling coffee into the cafetière. 'Now could it?'

Cassie sighed and gave up. She knew Nessa. They'd been best friends since their first day at Hillsdown Road when Nessa had got a detention for talking back to the teacher, and Cassie had got one too for giggling at Nessa's antics.

Nessa loved to share and discuss. She adored girl talk. And she was like a Rottweiler with a T-bone when it came to talking about sex. No way would she let the subject of Cassie's wild night drop until she'd got all the juicy details.

'Fine, all right.' Cassie grabbed the kettle, held it over the sink and wrenched on the tap. 'You got me. I did the wild thing with Jace Ryan last night.'

Nessa gave a deep chortle. 'I knew it.'

'How?' Cassie asked as she plonked the kettle onto its stand and flicked the switch on. Surely it couldn't be that obvious?

'Well, now, let me see,' Nessa said as her gaze roamed over Cassie's rapidly flushing face. 'Apart from that patch of whisker burn on your chin. There's that dazed look in your eyes that says your girly bits definitely got one heck of a wake-up call last night.'

'I see,' Cassie muttered, not too pleased with the reminder.

Her girly bits weren't doing denial nearly as well as she'd hoped when she'd walked out on Jace that morning. And Nessa's observation was not helping them get with the programme.

'So tell me,' Nessa said, pouring boiling water onto the grounds and infusing the small room with the tempting aroma of fresh coffee. 'Is that boy as mad, bad and dangerous to know as I remember him?'

Cassie lifted the pint bottle out of the fridge, added a splash of milk to the two Drama Queen mugs Nessa had placed on the counter top, and tried not to remember exactly how mad and bad Jace Ryan was in bed. 'He's certainly not a boy any more,' she murmured.

Nessa gave a joyous whoop, arranging the two apple pastries onto a plate. 'Hallelujah and amen to that!' She lifted her coffee, toasted Cassie with the china mug. 'It's about time you got yourself a man who knows what he's doing.' Picking up the plate, she led Cassie into the living room. They settled in their usual seats on the vintage fifties couch. 'So your Christmas is looking up, right? No more worries about missing he who shall not be named,' she hissed in a deliberately theatrical voice, using the nickname she'd coined for Lance, the morning Cassie had run round to her best friend to tell her the sordid details of what she'd discovered Lance and Tracy doing on her vintage couch. 'You got yourself a real man to snuggle up with on Christmas morning now.'

Cassie took a careful sip of her scalding coffee, and glanced over the rim of her mug at Nessa. 'Not exactly,' she said, and braced herself for the inevitable.

Nessa's perfectly plucked brows drew down in a sharp frown and she placed her mug on the coffee table. 'Why not exactly?'

'It was strictly a one-night deal.'

'You mean he doesn't want a repeat performance? Why not? Is there something wrong with him?' Nessa's voice was so full of indignation on Cassie's behalf she almost didn't want to admit the truth. Why not let Jace take the heat instead of her?

Unfortunately, the guilty flush burned in her cheeks before she could even open her mouth. Nessa's brows arrowed down further as suspicion flickered into her eyes.

Why couldn't she even tell a decent white lie? It was pathetic.

'Wait a minute, it's not him.' Nessa pointed an accusatory

finger at her. 'It's you, isn't it? Please tell me you're not still holding a candle to that tool Lance?'

'No, it's nothing like that. It's just…' Cassie hesitated. How did she explain her cowardice to Nessa, who was bolder than anyone she knew? 'Jace suggested continuing our fling, until he leaves on New Year's Day. But I don't want to do that.'

Nessa held up her hand, her eyes narrowing. 'Let me get this straight. The man offered you—' she did a quick calculation on her fingers '—twelve whole days of really amazing fornication. That'll see you right through your Christmas funk. And you turned him *down*?'

Cassie shifted in her seat. She hadn't exactly turned him down. She hadn't even been brave enough to do that. But there was absolutely no need to admit that to Nessa.

'Ness, I'm not ready for something like this.'

'But it's been nine months since you kicked out that no-good, lying—'

'I've slept with exactly two men in my life,' she interrupted, not wanting to hear another of Nessa's tirades against Lance. 'Well, three now,' she revised. 'And I'm not sure I…'

Cassie's fumbling explanation ground to a halt as Nessa sucked her teeth in derision.

'What?' Cassie said. 'Why do you look so fierce?'

'Right this second, I'm visualising what I'd like to do to that little cheater's nuts. This is all *his* fault,' Nessa snarled, sounding as fierce as she looked.

Cassie sighed. 'It's not his fault. Not any more. I got over him months ago.' The truth was it had been remarkably easy to let go of Lance. Once she'd kicked him out of her life it had become distressingly obvious that they had never been that good together. What had been much harder to let go had been all the romantic dreams she'd had of having a settled secure life with a man who loved her. Something her mother had never managed. Cassie had picked Lance for the male lead in her Happy Ever After plan because he'd been convenient and available and had seemed to want the same thing. She'd never looked beneath the surface of their relationship. Had taken the tepid attraction she felt for him, and the yearning to have a real commitment from a man who wouldn't break his promises, and turned their relationship in her mind into something it had never actually been.

'This goes further back than that,' Cassie admitted. 'Lance was just the trigger to make me realise something I've been refusing to admit to myself for years.'

'What's that?' Nessa said, clearly not getting Cassie's rambling explanation. Not all that surprising as she was only just starting to understand it herself.

'Remember how I always fell for my dad's lies too, Ness? Remember how excited I'd be when he said he was taking me to the zoo, or the cinema? I'd build all my hopes up, convinced this time would be different. And then I'd be devastated when he didn't show.'

'It isn't your fault your daddy was a tool too.'

'And David?' Cassie said. 'Remember him? The love of my life in art college who turned out not to be all that interested in me? Can't you see there's a pattern here? That has as much to do with me as them?'

'What pattern?'

'I've always been so gullible. So easily fooled by even the slightest show of affection. It's pathetic.'

Reaching across the coffee table, Nessa covered the hands Cassie had clenched in her lap. 'You're not gullible. You're sweet natured and optimistic. It's not a crime to always think the best of people.'

Cassie met her friend's steady, reassuring gaze. 'It is if you always end up letting yourself get hurt…I just don't want to tempt fate with a guy like Jace Ryan.'

'Damn.' Nessa shook her head. 'That is a shame, when he's so good in bed.'

Cassie sent her friend a weak smile. 'He's *too* good in bed. How can I guarantee I won't start getting more than just sexually attracted to him? I'll overdose on really amazing sex. And before you know it I'll be concocting yet another stupid fantasy that's going to end up biting me on the backside.'

Nessa threw up her hands, looking exasperated. 'Now wait a minute. Who says this couldn't lead to more? Stranger things have happened. Look at me and Terrence. We plain out hated each other at school and now we're engaged to be married.'

Nessa and Terrence hadn't hated each other at all; they'd just been in denial about their attraction for years. Something all their friends had figured out long before they had.

'Now who's the hopeless romantic?' Cassie arched her eyebrow. 'Quite apart from the fact Jace lives in another country.' She hesitated—or at least she had assumed he did, it was one of the many things they hadn't discussed during their all-night sex-fest. 'We're not talking about Terrence. We're talking about Jace the Ace. Do you have any idea how many girlfriends he got through at school? Because I do. He was my first major crush.' In fact he'd been her only crush. Once he'd been kicked out of school, she'd never got so obsessed again, because no one else had ever been able to live up to his perfection in her teenage eyes. 'Every other week, he'd have a new girlfriend hanging on his arm.' And every other week she'd gone through the torments of hell, as only a thirteen-year-old could, because that girl hadn't been her.

What a complete twit she'd been about men. Even then.

Nessa cradled her mug in her palms, scowling slightly. 'All right, I'll admit he may not be long-haul material. He certainly wasn't at school. But people change.'

'He hasn't,' Cassie mumbled, remembering the 'have I slept with you?' remark.

'Maybe. Maybe not. But one thing I do remember,' Nessa countered. 'He was always real careful not to be doing more than one girl at once. He was never a cheater,' she finished pointedly.

'Great!' Cassie puffed out a breath. 'So he's a serial monogamist. So what? He's still far too dangerous a man for me to get involved with at the moment. I'm through having my dreams trampled on…and I've got to take some of the responsibility for that. I've got to be proactive from now on, and make sure I only have realistic dreams.'

'Realistic dreams!' Nessa scoffed. 'Where's the fun in that? That sounds more boring than one of my Aunt Chantelle's Bible-study classes.'

'The fun is,' Cassie said mildly, 'with realistic dreams, you might actually have some hope of them coming true.'

CHAPTER TEN

THE loud buzz of the doorbell cut through the hum of the radio. Cassie's hand jerked and the newly reconstructed Sugar Plum took it on the nose again.

'Oh, for Pete's sake!' She glared at the white card, the intricate design of gossamer wings, willowy body and delicate features ruined a second time.

It had been two hours since Nessa had left and Cassie had set to work recreating her original drawing. After her chat with her best friend, her nerves had finally stopped jitterbugging enough for her to pick up her pen without risking another mishap. And to be honest she had to get this design done today. It was the twenty-first of December tomorrow. She had to get the cards printed this afternoon or she'd risk not getting them in the post in time for Christmas. Something she'd never failed to do before.

The doorbell buzzed longer and louder. Dumping the pen and picking up her washcloth, she marched to her front door. She had lots of friends and neighbours who often popped round to see her unannounced, but this was ridiculous. She'd put a sign on the door after Nessa left so she could draw in peace for the rest of the afternoon, and also because she'd wanted a bit of time to contemplate the revelations she'd finally discovered about herself in the last twenty-four hours.

Her body would always regret having to turn Jace down,

and it would have been wonderful to indulge herself over Christmas, but she was coming to terms with the fact that she'd done the right thing. Now all she had to do was persuade her hormones. And the best way to do that was to stop thinking about what she'd left behind in The Chesterton hotel suite this morning and start concentrating on her Christmas card design. Unfortunately her friends were not playing along.

Slipping the deadbolt lose, she wrenched open the door.

'Can't you read, you…?' Her hormones sprang into a brand new jitterbug as her gaze landed on the tall man standing on her doorstep with his hand braced against the door jamb and his pure green eyes glittering with annoyance.

'Jace? What are you doing here?' she whispered, her breath backing up in her lungs.

He straightened. 'What the hell do you *think* I'm doing here?' He marched past her into the flat, instantly making her tiny living room shrink to shoe-box size.

'I…' Her gaze devoured the broad shoulders accentuated by the black leather bomber jacket, the thick waves of dark brown hair brushed back in untidy furrows from that striking face. She was so shocked to see him. She didn't have a clue what to say. Why had he tracked her down? The bump in her heartbeat, which she had spent the day telling herself she had to ignore, kicked in again.

'You ran out on me!' He thrust his fingers through his hair, and she realised where the furrows had come from. 'I wake up and you're gone. No note. No nothing. How's that for a double standard?' He rested his hands on his waist, sent her an accusatory look. 'Because if a guy does that to a girl, it's considered incredibly tacky.'

He didn't just sound annoyed, she realised. She could hear the low growl of carefully controlled temper vibrating in his voice. And see the muscle clenching in his jaw. Had he been hurt by her silent departure? It didn't seem possible. But at the thought the little bump in her heartbeat took a sudden unexpected leap.

'I had to get home,' she said as guilt made the fine hairs on the back of her neck prickle. 'And you were fast asleep,' she added, struggling not to sound too defensive. She hadn't intended to hurt him. 'I didn't think you would want me to wake you.'

'Oh, come on!' He stepped forward, towering over her, his scowl darkening and the muscle in his jaw twitching. 'We used a whole box of condoms last night. I got so deep inside you that last time I could feel your heart beating. Don't start pretending you didn't know me well enough to at least give me the courtesy of a goodbye.'

The blunt words made heat pulse low in her abdomen. Colour exploded in her cheeks, but not before she realised something crucial. She hadn't hurt him. She'd insulted him. And that was entirely different.

'I'm sorry I left without saying goodbye,' she said carefully, feeling monumentally stupid. After everything she'd said to Nessa today, after everything she'd finally discovered about herself, how could she have been led astray by her romantic nature again so soon? 'I really didn't think you'd be that bothered.'

'Yeah, well, think again,' he snarled, so close now she could smell him, that devastating musk of man and soap. He cupped her head, drew her against him. She gasped, stunned by the unexpected contact, and the fierce arousal in his gaze, and then his mouth was on hers.

He thrust his tongue between her parted lips. Her hands braced against his chest, but instead of shoving him back, as she'd intended, her fingers curled into the soft sweater, the forceful strokes of his tongue igniting the heat at her core, and sending it burning through her system like a forest fire.

When he finally lifted his head, both of them were breathing heavily.

He dropped his hand, looking as shocked as she felt at the instant and violent attraction that had blazed to life in seconds.

Last night had been fun, flirty and intense, but only ever in a sexual sense. Why should a simple kiss feel more intimate?

'I'm sorry,' he murmured, shoving his hands into the pockets of his jacket. 'That was out of order. I guess I was more pissed off than I realised.'

'That's okay,' she said, feeling both stunned and wary. Although it wasn't okay. Not really, but not for the reasons he thought. She'd welcomed the kiss, her body reacting instinctively to it. So how on earth was she going to get her jitterbugging hormones back under control now? And how was she going to persuade herself that she didn't care what she was giving up, when her body would probably never stop reminding her?

'It was rude of me to leave without saying anything,' she whispered.

He propped his butt on the edge of the sofa. Hitched his shoulders as he shoved his fists deeper into his pockets. 'You never gave me an answer.' A crooked smile lifted his lips. 'I guess I'm not used to women doing that. I wasn't expecting you to be gone this morning.'

It was as she suspected. His ego had been dented. Nothing more dramatic than that.

He levered himself off the sofa. 'Let me ask again, the way I should have done when I walked in. Instead of giving you a hard time.'

And a kiss that had nearly blown the top of her head off, Cassie added silently as he took one hand out of his pocket and touched her cheek.

She shivered, the contact as electric as it had been a moment ago, even though he was barely touching her.

He stroked his thumb across her lips. 'How do you feel about hanging out with me, till I go back to New York on New Year's Day?'

'You live in New York?' she said a bit inanely.

'Haven't I mentioned that already?'

She shook her head.

He smiled. 'Seems like we've got some catching up to do. We've kind of done this thing backwards, haven't we?'

What thing? They didn't have a thing, she thought, her panic button tripping again.

'So do I get an answer this time?' he prompted.

But he didn't sound nearly as sure of himself as he had yesterday. The thought made her feel a little less wary of him. That cast-iron control had slipped when he'd kissed her. If only for a moment. And it made him seem a tiny bit less overpowering.

She took a steady breath and opted to tell him the truth. 'My answer is, I'm not sure.'

He tilted his head to one side, rubbed one of her curls between his thumb and forefinger. 'What's not to be sure about?' he asked.

'I don't know you.'

'We'll get to know each other.' His lips curved into a rueful smile. 'As much as I'd like to spend the next ten days making nonstop love to you, even I have my limits. And we'll probably have to eat occasionally. Which means we'll no doubt have to talk to each other.'

She stepped back, tucked her hands into the back pockets of her jeans, impossibly tempted by the chance to get to know him better. But she would have to tell him the rest first.

She met his eyes. 'I got hurt. Nine months ago. When my

last relationship ended. And I don't want to get involved with anyone right now.'

'Involved?' His eyebrows shot up. 'How does ten days of small talk and great sex equal involved?'

'It doesn't,' she corrected quickly. She didn't want him thinking she was a romantic fool. Because she wasn't. Not any more. 'I know it doesn't. Which is a good thing. Because that's definitely not what I want.'

He slipped his hand round her waist, hauled her against him. 'Then there isn't a problem.' He kissed her, lingering on her lips this time, making her sex ache and her breasts swell and tighten. 'Is there?'

Could it really be that simple?

The crooked smile became even more charming. 'You know, Cassidy, you're being a bit of a girl about this.'

'That's possibly because I am a girl,' she pointed out, not sure whether to laugh at the statement or be affronted.

'I know.' He kissed her again. 'And that's a very good point. But why don't I give you a guy's perspective?' he said, as if he were humouring her. 'To help clarify things.'

'Okay,' she said, intrigued to see where this was going.

'The truth is,' he began, 'I'm not the sort of guy anyone gets *involved* with. And for a very good reason. I'm not remotely reliable,' he said, not sounding in the least bit ashamed of his lack of constancy.

'You got involved with your wife, didn't you?' she countered.

He cleared his throat. 'She's my ex-wife. Which sort of proves my point.'

'Fair enough.'

'So as I was saying, before I was so rudely interrupted,' he admonished, his eyes twinkling. 'You don't need to worry about me expecting more from this relationship than you want to give me. Because I can guarantee you. I won't want more than I've asked for, which is—'

'Great sex and small talk,' she finished for him.

'Exactly!' he said as if she were a brilliant student and he the teacher. 'You see, guys are very straightforward. We want what we say on the tin. There is hardly ever a hidden subtext. And there certainly isn't one here.'

'And what does your tin say?' she asked, unable to stifle a grin.

The man was a complete rogue where women were concerned. And while she probably shouldn't find his lack of scruples refreshing, somehow she did. David and Lance had both pretended to be something they weren't. Namely dependable and reliable and in the market for a real relationship when they never had been. While Jace, for all his wicked ways, had been honest about what he wanted. And what he didn't.

Nessa had told her he wasn't a cheater. And she'd been spot on.

He smiled as the desire in his eyes intensified. He pressed against her, the rigid arousal making her hormones do a very happy dance indeed. 'My tin says that I don't get involved.' He sank his fingers into her hair, framing her face. 'But I do have some other fine qualities that we can explore at our leisure for eleven whole days.'

He lowered his head, until his lips hovered over hers. 'What do you say, Cassidy? Are you gonna go for it or not? Ladies' choice.'

As arousal sprinted through her system and her body swayed instinctively into his, Cassie knew she was lost, the promise of pleasure in his eyes, and the feel of the thick ridge outlined against her abdomen, too tempting to resist a second time.

Circling his waist and lifting on tiptoe, she closed the distance and settled her lips on his. The kiss was slow and easy this time, but a smouldering heat built in her belly that quickly threatened to rage out of control.

He pulled back, his ragged breathing matching hers. 'I'll take that as a yes, then?'

She nodded, her tongue too numb to speak—and her mind too dazed with passion to consider refusing. Optimism flooded through her as he bent to devour the pulse point in her neck, then grasped her thigh to hook her leg over his hip. He pushed her back against the wall, ground the heavy weight of his sex into the juncture of her thighs, making moisture release in a rush through the denim of her jeans.

She arched against him, pushing herself into the hardness, desperate to feel it inside her again.

But when the heart bump came this time, the panic didn't follow.

This was about sex. Really amazing sex. And nothing more. She'd examined the pitfalls and knew what they were, so she could guard against them. But she wouldn't even have to.

She'd tried to complicate something that was remarkably simple.

Those telltale bumps in her heartbeat had been caused by the intensity of her arousal, that was all. And she'd panicked. But there was nothing to panic about. And there never had been.

She could have her candy…and eat it too. Because candy was all it was ever meant to be. And she knew that now.

Clasping her hips in his hands, he lifted her. 'Wrap your legs round my waist.'

She did as he demanded, delirious with the sharp, insistent need she no longer had to deny.

He carried into her bedroom, dumped her on the bed, then got to work on the buttons of her jeans.

'At last.' He let out a satisfied sigh as he eased his hands under the waistband, pushed the denims over her hips. 'Let's get this party started.'

And he did.

'Is that the right time?' Jace squinted at the clock on the wall above Cassie's desk. Easing his arm from around her shoulders, he sat upright in her small double bed. 'It can't be two o'clock already.' When he'd come charging out of the hotel an hour ago, determined to give Cassie a roasting for running out on him, he hadn't checked the time. Why hadn't he checked?

'Yes, it is,' Cassie murmured, sitting up beside him, her voice husky as she clutched the duvet to her breasts. 'What's wrong?'

He ruthlessly controlled the surge of heat at the sight of the soft flesh. He knew why he hadn't stopped to check the time. Because he hadn't been able to see past his lust, and the spike of temper that had gripped him when he'd woken up to find Cassie gone.

Damn it all to hell, he needed to focus now. Getting out of the bed, he grabbed his boxers off the floor, tugged them on. 'I have a meeting I was supposed to be at an hour ago.'

'Can you ring them?' she said, sounding concerned. 'Will it be a problem for you?'

He grabbed his trousers, shoved his legs into them, then whipped his sweater off the floor and pulled it over his head. 'I don't have to call. It's not a problem,' he said, knowing it wasn't. Not in a business sense. The buyers would be happy to wait a week to see him, let alone an hour. But that didn't stem his irritation with himself.

When was the last time a woman had distracted him from his business? Even for an hour. Never. Not even during his marriage. It was the thing that had always upset Helen the most. That he insisted on putting the business first.

But he hadn't given a thought to his business commitments today when he'd been showering and then getting The Chesterton's concierge to find out where the cab Cassie had booked at the front desk had taken her.

And while he'd got what he'd wanted—namely Cassie agreeing to be his playmate for the next week or so—he didn't much like the ridiculous way he'd behaved when he got to her flat either. The minute he'd seen her again, the combination of lust and longing and anger had got all tangled up inside him—and he hadn't been able to distinguish them. He'd discovered at an early age the value of keeping your emotions under wraps. And as a teenager, the even greater value of being able to deflect and deny the more destructive ones. Anger was definitely one of those emotions that was better controlled.

But for some damn reason, he hadn't been able to control it today. He needed to get out of Cassie's apartment and get to the meeting. Indulging himself with her was going to be fun over the next week or so. But he needed a little distance now to get this fling in perspective. He'd got what he wanted. And he wasn't going to worry too much about why he'd wanted it so much.

The sound of her sobbing out her release as her sex tightened around him ten minutes ago was all the explanation he needed for that.

'I'll have to dash,' he said, sitting on the edge of the bed to pull on his socks and boots. Having a little time out would be good for both of them. His smile edged up as his heartbeat calmed. Especially as they had well over a week of really amazing sex ahead of them.

He twisted round, laid his hand on her knee. 'Why don't you pack a bag? I'll send a car over and see you at the hotel for dinner.'

'Pack a bag?' Her brows lowered in a puzzled frown. 'Why do I need to pack a bag?'

He sent her a level look, tried not to overreact to the genuine look of confusion. 'Because you're moving in till New Year's Day, remember?'

Her teeth tugged on her bottom lip. 'But I—'

He silenced her by pressing a finger to her lips. 'Cassie, it's easier this way.' He made an effort to lighten his voice, add a little of the charm that he was so famous for. The charm that had pretty much deserted him once already today. 'They have room service. And a much bigger bed.'

Her cheeks pinkened prettily. 'I suppose you're right,' she said, still sounding unsure.

'I know I'm right.' Then he pushed his advantage. 'Just out of interest, how many flings like this have you had?' he asked.

She looked down, the pink in her cheeks turning to a vivid red. 'None,' she said.

He quashed the odd tightening in his chest, which made no sense at all. Why should he care if she'd done this before or not? He'd had plenty of flings; in fact, that was pretty much all he'd ever had. Even during his marriage, he'd never cared about Helen's past sex life. So he didn't get to care whether Cassie had done this before or not. But still her inexperience, and the comment she'd made about the end of her previous relationship, bothered him in a way he couldn't quite figure out.

He lifted her chin with his finger. 'Then you'll have to take it from me that I know how these things work. And really amazing sex is a lot easier with room service.' And in an anonymous location, where no one's personal space was involved, he thought silently.

'Okay, I'll pack a bag,' she said.

He ignored the rush of relief.

It was only because she'd been a harder sell than he would

have expected. But he'd got what he wanted now. All he had to do was enjoy it.

'But I have plans for Christmas Day,' she added. 'And shopping and stuff to do before then.'

'Not a problem,' he said, curving his hand round her neck and pulling her to him for a long, languid kiss that would have to last him till dinnertime. 'I've got business commitments myself.' When he lifted his lips, the blush of embarrassment had turned to the flush of arousal. Just the way he liked it. 'I won't hold you prisoner at The Chesterton.'

She gave a quick, artlessly sexy smile. 'Promise?'

He chuckled. 'See you in a couple of hours.'

But as he strode through the living room, grabbed his jacket off the sofa and then let himself out of the tiny flat he knew it wasn't a promise he was likely to keep. He wasn't going to be letting her out of his sight for the next few days; whatever plans she might have, he'd just have to persuade her to adjust them. He'd speak to his PA after this afternoon's meeting and get her to reschedule the rest of his own commitments until after Christmas.

He'd been denying his libido too long; the way he'd over-reacted this morning was proof of that. His sudden inability to control his emotions had all been tied in with his lust. The next few days would be about working that need out of his system. And showing Cassie what he suspected she might have been missing in her sex life too. Once they'd both got what they wanted out of their affair, Cassie wouldn't have any more of an effect on him than all his other flings.

Cassie climbed out of bed as she heard the front door slam behind Jace. And pushed aside the spurt of hurt and disappointment that he'd rushed off so quickly.

What was she upset about? She'd agreed that their liaison

was about great sex. He wasn't making a commitment for anything more than that and neither was she.

And while his suggestion that she come and stay at the hotel—correction, his insistence that she come and stay at the hotel—had made her panic button pop again, she could see now it was the practical solution.

Grabbing her clothes up off the floor, she dropped the duvet and began to get dressed. Not only that, but the hotel suite was beautiful. And it would be much easier to remember this whole thing as some glorious sexual fantasy afterwards if they didn't spend too much time in her flat. Not that it would be a problem. But she didn't want to store up memories of him here. It would seem too much like a proper relationship when it wasn't.

And she'd be free to come and go at her leisure. Which she would definitely have to do. Because while she'd done her usual copious research for all the Christmas presents she had to buy, she hadn't actually got round to buying any yet.

Sitting back at her easel, she lifted up the Sugar Plum Fairy design and scrunched up the card. Then drew out a new card and started drawing. She'd finish her Christmas card design, get Manny at the printing shop round the corner to do a rush job, then post them before she packed up some stuff and went round to The Chesterton later.

There was no big rush, especially as Jace wouldn't even be there.

This was a casual affair. That was how he was treating it, and how she would treat it too. No blowing it out of proportion in any way. And no getting upset about him having to rush off to a business meeting, especially as she had lots of things to rush off and do in the next few days too.

CHAPTER ELEVEN

'It's Sunday!' Cassie stared at the Sunday papers she'd just noticed folded on the coffee table, the spoon of muesli poised in mid-air. 'It can't be.'

Jace glanced up from the plate of Cumberland sausage and eggs he'd been tucking into. 'That's correct. Sunday usually comes right after Saturday.'

Cassie plopped the spoon back into her bowl. 'But Sunday is Christmas Eve.'

'Is it?' Jace said, apparently unconcerned as he sliced into his sausage.

Cassie blinked. Watching him as he chewed the meat, then swallowed, her mind having gone completely blank. How could this have happened? She'd arrived at his hotel suite on the night of the twentieth of December. And now it was the morning of the twenty-fourth!

Which meant, even with her atrocious maths skills, that they'd spent three whole days cocooned in his hotel suite. Ordering in room service and indulging in an orgy of sexual pleasures, fulfilling every prurient fantasy she'd ever had, not to mention a great deal more that she'd never even dreamed of.

'I can't believe it's nearly Christmas Day already,' she murmured, feeling disorientated.

Three whole days. It didn't seem possible she could have

spent all that time doing nothing but making mad, passionate love to Jace Ryan.

The small talk he'd promised hadn't really materialised. Not in the way she would have hoped. He'd asked her a lot of questions about her work as an illustrator and she'd learned a little about his web design business, which was clearly very successful. But the few times she'd strayed into more personal territory, he'd clammed up and then distracted her. Mostly with sex. And she had forced herself not to take it personally. And not to push. Revelling instead in the passion he stirred so easily.

He shrugged, sent her a suggestive smile that had the heat pooling low in her abdomen. 'We've been busy.'

Cassie's skin heated as he pierced her with that hungry look again.

Pushing back from the breakfast table, she tightened the tie on her robe. 'I should shower and get dressed. I've got a lot to do today.' Three whole days had gone by in a haze of lust and passion and she hadn't even noticed.

As she went to walk past him he snagged her wrist. 'How about I come in and scrub your back for you?'

She tugged her hand free, dismayed by the way her pulse punched his thumb and her hormones instantly jitterbugged into overdrive as if leaping for joy at the prospect.

They'd made love less than half an hour ago when he'd woken her up to tell her breakfast had arrived, his fingers had started stroking and before she'd known it she'd been rocketing to orgasm while she was still barely awake. And just like all the other times they'd made love, she'd felt the clutch in her chest, the tightening in her heart muscle as he'd carried her into the suite's living room and plopped her down in front of her breakfast. And she'd steadfastly ignored the bump. But even she couldn't ignore the fact any longer that her behaviour was veering out of her control.

If this was all just about sex, why couldn't she seem to get enough of him? And why was the need inside her increasing with each passing day instead of abating?

'I'd better shower alone this morning,' she said, remembering how last morning's shared shower had ended.

'Hey.' He stood up as she turned to go, circled both of her wrists with his fingers to hold her in place. 'What's the matter? You look kind of spooked.'

Spooked was putting it mildly, she realised as she looked into his pure green eyes, and realised she didn't actually know any more about him than she had four days ago. 'I think I'm just getting a little stir crazy,' she said. That had to be it. She simply wasn't used to a physical relationship of this intensity. And it would probably be good to dial it down today. Plus she really did have a lot to do. She had a ton of Christmas presents to buy. 'We haven't left the hotel suite since Wednesday night,' she reasoned.

'True.' He lifted his hands to frame her face, leaned in to give her a quick kiss. 'I guess I haven't kept my promise, have I?' he said sheepishly.

'What promise?'

'Not to keep you a prisoner here.'

She felt herself flush, and her heart clenched again as she sent him a crooked smile. She forced the feeling of elation down. *Don't be daft.* The intensity of the relationship in the last three days had been purely sexual. His desire to spend time with her had no more significance than fulfilling a physical urge. For both of them. And the fact that her body still responded to him with such intensity was proof of that. For goodness' sake, she'd just established the fact that she hadn't got to know him, as she'd planned. And that hadn't just been his doing. She hadn't pressed because she'd been happy with the way things were. Because she'd been determined not to read anything more into their intimacy.

'I've enjoyed it,' she said. 'But I'll have to break out today. I've got a ton of shopping to do.'

His hands trailed down her arms, gripped her wrists for a second then let go.

'I guess that means I'm going to have to let you go for the day,' he said, sounding genuinely disappointed.

'Not necessarily,' she heard herself reply. 'You could always come with me,' she added, before she lost her nerve.

While she totally understood this was about great sex and nothing more, the compelling desire to spend time with him outside the hotel suite was unstoppable.

It would give them the chance to talk properly. And there were so many things she'd become curious about in the last four days. His failed marriage, his past, how the moody boy from a 'bad home' she remembered from school had become such a charismatic and successful man. All things she hadn't had the chance to ask about. Maybe that was why the heart bumps kept getting worse. Because she wanted to know more about him, and the more she didn't know, the more he avoided giving her that information, the more vulnerable she felt.

If he came shopping with her, she'd be able to quiz him without him being able to distract her quite so easily.

She dismissed the niggling little voice that told her she might be straying into dangerous territory. She'd become more sexually intimate with this man than she had with any other man. He knew things about her body that no other man had ever even bothered to discover. How could it be wrong to want to know a bit more about him? It didn't mean she would lose sight of her objectives. They'd already set out exactly what this relationship entailed and what it didn't. And they'd been busy reinforcing that point in the most delicious way possible for three whole days. So where was the harm in satisfying a little of her curiosity about him now?

Jacob Ryan had been a fascinating enigma ever since she'd

had a crush on him at school. He'd always been so taciturn and surly then. And while he had acquired a layer of relaxed easy-going charm as an adult, she couldn't help wondering if traces of that angry boy still existed, or if he had disappeared for good.

Surely this would be the perfect opportunity to dispel her fascination with him once and for all. Because she had an awful feeling that all the great sex they'd been having might have started to reawaken that stupid crush. Which would explain all the heart bumps. And that could not be a good thing.

'Nah, you go ahead,' he said, sitting back down and picking up the paper. 'I'll contact my PA. I should schedule some of those meetings today while you're not here to distract me.'

'But, Jace, that's silly. It's Sunday. And it's Christmas Eve. No one will be able to meet today. And we could have lunch out together.' She hurried on, trying not to sound too eager, the opportunity to have some of her curiosity satisfied suddenly irresistible. 'And don't you have any Christmas shopping to do?'

Jace stared at Cassie and kept his mouth firmly shut, before he did something really daft, like agreeing to go with her. Ever since she'd turned up at the hotel four nights ago, her small wheel-around suitcase in her hand and a shy but eager smile on her face, he hadn't let her out of his sight. In fact, he'd barely let her out of his bed. The plan had been to seduce them both into a coma, overdose on great sex for a few days and get the driving need to have her out of his system. Parts A and B of his plan had worked out great—a bit too great. Because part C had clearly been a dead loss. If not, why would he have the driving urge to stop her going out as soon as she had suggested it?

The woman was becoming an addiction. An addiction that

all the really amazing sex seemed to be making worse, not better.

Luckily he had the perfect excuse not to accept her invitation. He folded the paper, dumped it back on the coffee table. 'Believe me, Cassidy. You don't want me along.'

'Yes, I do,' she said, earnestly. 'Why wouldn't I?'

'Because I hate shopping. I won't be good company.'

'Why do you hate shopping?'

He shrugged; this bit at least was easy. 'There's always crowds of people and too much stuff to choose from and it takes for ever. Before you know it you've lost the will to live over a rack full of suits. I'd rather be kicked in the...' He paused when Cassie winced. 'I'd rather be kicked somewhere a guy definitely does not want to be kicked,' he finished, deciding to spare her the graphic visual.

'What is it about guys and shopping?' she said, exasperation edging her voice. 'It's the eighth wonder of the world if you do it right.'

'I do do it right,' he said flatly. 'I do all my shopping online.'

She didn't just wince this time, she flinched. 'That's awful. How can you buy clothes on a computer? Especially designer ones. You've got to try them on, see how they hang. What the cut's like. You can't tell that from a picture and a list of measurements.'

'If I don't like it, I send it back. Get a refund.'

'Which means standing for hours in a post office queue. Personally, I'd rather take my chances at the shops.'

He sent her a level look. 'I don't do post office queues.'

'How can you send it back if—?'

'Put it this way.' He stopped her in mid-argument. 'One of the reasons I worked so hard to earn my first million was so I could send someone else to queue at the post office.'

She dropped back on her heels, an adorable crease of consternation lining her brow.

'And so I would never have to enter a department store again in this lifetime,' he added forcefully. 'Especially not in the West End on Christmas Eve. It'll be my worst nightmare,' he said, determined to keep that fact front and centre. He didn't do shopping, even with someone as cute and sexy as Cassie.

'No, it won't,' she said, clearly not prepared to be beaten. 'It won't even take that long.'

'How so?'

'I happen to be a champion shopper.'

Yeah, right. Most women didn't even know what that was.

'I'm getting the impression from that sceptical look that you don't believe me,' she said. 'How about I make you a bet that we get everything done in under an hour?'

'How many people do you have to get stuff for?' he asked judiciously.

'Umm.' She curled her plump bottom lip under her teeth as if she were counting up the number in her head. 'Ten. No.' Her eyes met his, the bright light of excitement in them almost tangible. 'Eleven.'

'Eleven presents in under an hour? In the West End? On Christmas Eve? For a woman who loves to shop?' he clarified.

She nodded enthusiastically.

'Not possible.' This had to be the sucker bet to end all sucker bets. 'And what do I get if you don't manage it?'

'Hmm, let me think.' She pressed the tip of her finger to her mouth, then leaned forward and touched his chest. Her nail trailed down over one nipple, across his ribs, down his abs and stopped just short of his belly button where his robe closed. She sent him a coy smile. 'I'm sure I can think of something that you'll enjoy,' she said, her voice husky with provocation.

Despite his recent climax, he could feel himself rising to attention. He wrapped his hand around her finger, lifted it off his belly. The little tease. She was going to pay for that.

'You're on,' he declared. 'But once the hour's up we head straight back here and get naked.'

One hour of shopping seemed like a small price to pay for the fantasies he was already conjuring to go with her sultry smile. And once they were back in the suite, everything would be back where he wanted it.

'You're assuming you're going to win,' she said sweetly. 'But when you don't, when the hour's up, I get to take you to lunch.' The sultry smile became decidedly smug. 'And we get to have a proper conversation. About something other than sex,' she added.

He smiled back. It had been fairly easy to distract her up to now. So even if the unthinkable happened and he lost the bet, that didn't scare him. 'All right, you're on.'

He dragged her into his arms to seal the deal, but she wrestled out of his embrace and tapped a finger to his nose. 'Not so fast, Ryan. No kissing until we're in public.' She lifted her eyebrows. 'I know all your tricks.'

He chuckled as she dashed off to the bathroom. 'Not yet you don't,' he murmured, feeling pretty smug himself. He'd managed to manoeuvre her into only spending an hour away from his bed today.

If this was an addiction, he had the will power to overcome it, once he set his mind to it. He'd overcome much bigger weaknesses to get what he wanted.

But there was no need to go cold turkey. At least not today.

Jace was feeling a lot less smug an hour later as Cassie walked back towards him with her latest purchase clutched in her fist and a triumphant smile on her face.

'What's the tally now?' he muttered.

She held the bag up. 'Jill's present makes eight.'

Jace glanced at his watch and groaned. They were only thirty-five minutes into their shopping marathon, and she'd already got over two-thirds of her stash.

She laughed at his frown. 'Regretting taking me on, Ryan?'

'You're not there yet, sweet cheeks,' he countered, but his confidence about winning the bet was ebbing fast. He slung the three bags of purchases she'd given him to carry over his shoulder. Although, funnily enough, he hadn't been nearly as bored or frustrated as he would have expected. In fact, watching Cassie shop was nothing short of fascinating.

She really was a champion shopper. Unlike with any other woman he'd had the misfortune to shop with, she seemed to know exactly what she wanted and where to get it. She'd attacked Oxford Street with military precision, avoiding the big chain stores, and instead using a string of smaller independent shops and boutiques mostly dotted on the side streets whose merchandise she seemed to have expert knowledge of. She didn't browse, she went straight to the counter and described exactly what she wanted. He'd also noticed that her purchases were incredibly well thought out and individual. If he didn't know better, he could have sworn she'd actually researched this trip.

As they walked out of the chocolaterie and back towards the throbbing activity of Oxford Street he noticed her open her bag and peek at something inside. He'd noticed her doing that a couple of times already. Snagging the leather bag from behind, he whisked it out of her hands and off her shoulder. 'Let's have a look in there.'

'Hey, what are you…?' she yelped.

'What have you got? A secret weapon?' Spotting the piece of paper she'd been reading, he whipped it out of her bag.

'Give that back.' She made a jump for it, but he held the paper easily out of reach.

'Damn, it *is* a secret weapon.' He stared at the handwritten list, which had annotations and notes, hand-drawn maps and several intricate little drawings jotted all over it. The thing was a work of art. She must have spent hours on it. A weird feeling of weightlessness lifted his stomach at the thought that she'd gone to so much trouble. That anyone would go to that much trouble. Over a bunch of Christmas presents.

'What is this?' he asked.

'Give it back. It's my Christmas list,' she said, embarrassment turning her cheeks a bright shade of pink. She looked so damn cute and determined, the weightlessness increased.

'How comes I never knew this about you?' he teased, pushing the sentimental thought to one side. It was a shopping list, for goodness' sake, not the Declaration of Independence or the Magna Carta.

'Knew what?' she said, swiping the list out of his hand when he dropped his arm.

'That you're anal.'

'I am *not* anal,' she declared, stuffing the list back into her bag. 'I'm organised. And where Christmas shopping is concerned, it pays to be organised.'

'I get it.' The drop in his stomach lifted. 'You write the list so you don't overspend, right?' That had to be the reason why she'd gone to all that trouble. It was so long since he'd had to buy on a budget he'd forgotten what it was like.

'No.' She stared at him as if he were witless. 'I go to the trouble of writing a list so I don't get the wrong thing. Getting people the right present takes work and consideration. I know it's a cliché but it really is the thought that counts.'

If that were the case her friends would be rich, he thought, feeling uncomfortable again.

He couldn't quite believe how much time and effort she'd clearly put into the process. This wasn't about being a shopaholic. It was about actually caring about people enough to want to get them something they'd really like. The minute the thought registered, the weightlessness returned and the uncomfortable feeling got worse.

'I like going that extra mile for the people I care about,' she said doggedly. 'Because I know they'll go that extra mile for me.' She looped her arm through his. 'Now stop trying to waste time, we've still got three presents to go and they're the most important.' She headed across Oxford Street, the fairy lights of Selfridges' facade making her hair sparkle. 'And for that we need the big guns.'

As she dragged him into the legendary department store he realised that he'd never cared about anyone enough to want to get them something special for Christmas. And no one had ever really cared that much about him.

And it hadn't bothered him.

Right up until he'd got suckered into going Christmas shopping with Cassie Fitzgerald.

'See, I told you I was a champion shopper,' Cassie said as she pushed onto the bench seat and settled the bags of presents she'd purchased under the dinner table, the sense of accomplishment making her feel more than a little smug.

She folded her arms and waited for Jace to take the seat opposite. She had a lot to be satisfied about. Not only had she got all her shopping done in under an hour, she'd also managed to awaken Jace to the true joys of retail therapy. Despite all his earlier protestations, she thought he'd actually quite enjoyed the experience. She'd asked his opinion so many times that after a while he'd been forced to get involved. And by the time they'd got to Selfridges, instead of the usual monosyllabic answers, they'd had a very useful discussion about the merits of different brands of men's sportswear. She'd wanted to get Nessa's fiancé Terrence something really good to train in, but didn't know a thing about tracksuit brands—what was in at the moment and what wasn't—and Jace had been surprisingly informative. She doubted he would appreciate her pointing that out now though. Because, while it had been touch-and-go for the last ten minutes of her allotted hour, when she'd wasted precious seconds agonising over whether to get Nessa the amethyst pendant or the faux sapphire, Jace had lost the bet. And he didn't seem to be a very good loser.

Jace slid the tray holding the steaming pastrami on rye sandwiches they'd purchased at the counter, and sent her a disgruntled look. 'Don't rub it in, Fitzgerald. If I'd known you were going to cheat, I would never have made the bet.'

'How did I cheat?' she exclaimed, having to fake her outrage, as she was enjoying her victory too much.

'That list.' He sat down and lifted the plates off the tray. 'I didn't know you'd been in training for weeks. If I had...' His voice trailed off.

She grinned. 'Gee, Ryan. Sore loser much?' she teased, unable to resist rubbing it in, just a tad.

His lips tilted up as he slathered mustard on his pastrami. 'Gee, Fitzgerald,' he countered. 'Smug winner much?' He took a bite into the sandwich with relish. 'Damn, that's good,' he said, wiping his mouth with a napkin. 'It tastes like the real thing.'

'It *is* the real thing,' Cassie replied as she sliced into her own sandwich to make the hearty slabs of rye bread a bit more manageable. 'This is Selfridges Food Hall.'

'I know that,' he replied, his voice gruff, but his eyes bright with humour as he took a swig from his bottle of mineral water. 'I've just wasted five minutes of my life debating the merits of Marmite chocolate, remember.'

She gave a light little laugh. 'Stop pretending you weren't severely tempted to buy a bar.'

He sent her a smouldering look that promised retribution at a later date as he took another bite.

'And you should be looking on the bright side,' she added, watching him devour his sandwich. 'Now I've done all my shopping, we can devote some time to doing yours,' she announced, hoping that he hadn't done his already. All the guys she had ever known did the majority of their Christmas shopping at the last second. 'You have a champion shopper at your disposal to help. And I know Selfridges and Oxford Street like the back of my hand. All you have to do is tell me who the person is, what they like and don't like and I'll be able to locate the perfect present within a mile radius, I guarantee it,' she said, her enthusiasm increasing. Seeing whom he bought gifts for would provide a fascinating insight into his private life without her having to probe. 'Really, I should charge for my services,' she finished.

She picked up her sandwich and took a bite as he swallowed the last of his down. He took another swig of his water, swiped the spot of mustard from the corner of his lips, then dumped his napkin on the empty plate, a considering look in her eyes.

'No need,' he said. 'I don't have any shopping.'

She gulped the bite of her sandwich down, trying not to be too disappointed by the news. 'That's a first. I've never met a man who has all his Christmas shopping done before Christmas Eve.'

'I haven't done it already.' He tapped his thumb on the side of his plate. 'I just don't do any.'

'What do you mean you don't do any?' she said, disappointment replaced by shock as her eyes widened. 'What about your family? Your friends? Don't you get them presents?'

He didn't seem fazed by the question, even though the very thought of not buying anything for people you loved was unthinkable to her.

He shrugged, the movement stiff. 'I don't have any family. And my friends know I don't like to receive anything, so they don't expect anything in return.'

'But how do you celebrate Christmas, then?' she asked, shock giving way to astonishment and an odd sense of sadness. She didn't have any family any more either, not since her mother had died. Her father was still alive, but she'd given up on him years ago. Even so she'd filled the gap with a wide circle of friends—and Christmas had always been the perfect time to catch up and enjoy each other's company. She loved the ritual of the season, the sense of love and companionship she shared with the important people in her life. How could you really participate in that without the giving and receiving of gifts? They didn't have to be expensive. She'd splurged this year because she'd had a couple of successful commissions and had begun to make a name for herself as an illustrator. But she could still remember previous years when all she'd been able to afford were home-made stuff or bargain gifts, and she'd still enjoyed doing her Christmas list just as much.

'Simple,' he said, his voice devoid of emotion. 'I don't celebrate Christmas.'

'You don't...' She paused, nonplussed by the blank look on his face.

Of course she knew there were people who hated Christmas, usually for specific reasons. It could be a stressful time, especially when your family life wasn't great. And whatever Ms Tremall had meant all those years ago by a 'bad home' she suspected Jace's family life might have been the opposite of great. But he didn't sound as if he hated Christmas, just as if he were indifferent to it. Which somehow seemed even sadder.

'But you must have celebrated it with your wife?' she asked, her skin flushing a little at the boldness of the question.

She hadn't meant to probe. She knew however curious she

was about his past, she didn't really have the right to ask him personal questions, but instead of clamming up as he had before, he simply leant back in his chair and studied her for a moment.

'We weren't married that long,' he commented. 'You know, if there's something you want to ask me about my marriage, why don't you just ask?'

Her skin heated. Had she been that obvious? Clearly, she had been if the implacable look in his eyes was anything to go by.

But despite feeling exposed, despite knowing she'd been caught asking something that was none of her business, and despite being certain that Jace's offer to ask him about his marriage was disingenuous, the rapid ticks of Cassie's heartbeat rose in her throat and she recalled the look in his ex-wife's face five days ago. And admitted to herself that the naked pain in Helen's gaze had niggled at the back of her mind ever since that day.

'All right, I have got something to ask,' she said softly, forcing the question out before she could stop herself. 'Did you love Helen when you married her?'

CHAPTER TWELVE

'DID I *love* her?' Jace choked out a laugh, and wanted to kick himself for being so stupid.

Why had he opened himself up to this? He always kept things casual with women he slept with, and opening up the can of worms that was his marriage could get a little heavy. He should probably just lie. He'd done it before, because it had been the easy way out.

But somehow the earnestness in Cassie's expression and the gently asked question made him hesitate. And then he really wanted to kick himself, because, however easy or convenient it was, he knew he couldn't lie to her. Which was all wrapped up in watching her spend an hour devoting so much time and energy to getting presents for people he didn't even know. He now knew just how sweet and genuine she really was—which meant it would probably be wise to let her know exactly the kind of man he was.

They had already agreed about the terms of their relationship, and that was great. But he'd seen the way she'd looked at him, knew that he was a first for her when it came to no-strings sex—and he didn't want any confusion about what was really going on here.

'No, I didn't love her,' he admitted flatly, careful not to put any inflection into his voice. The facts spoke for themselves. He watched the look of confusion cross her expressive face.

He could have added in his defence that as far as he was concerned there was no such thing as love. But once you said that, women had a bad habit of trying to persuade you otherwise. Or worse, find out why you thought that. Something he wasn't about to get into. Because if the subject of his marriage was a can of worms he didn't like prising open, the subject of his childhood was a whole barrel of them.

'But if you didn't love her, why did you marry her?' she asked.

The delicious pastrami sandwich he had eaten sat in his stomach like a ball of lead.

He swallowed heavily and looked down at his plate. He probably should have expected the question, but it didn't make it any easier to answer.

'Her father provided the start-up investment for Artisan. He found out I'd been screwing Daddy's little girl and gave me an ultimatum. Either I make an honest woman of her, or he was pulling the finance.' He met her eyes as he said the words. He'd done what he had to do to get out. And okay, he'd made mistakes. Succumbing to Helen's questionable charms being a whopper. But he'd paid the price for his stupidity and his lack of restraint. So why should he feel guilty about it now?

'Basically, I married her for her father's money. And not all that surprisingly, the marriage only lasted six months.'

Cassie didn't look disgusted or even all that judgemental about what he'd told her, but annoyingly he still felt the need to justify his actions. Not something he'd ever done before. 'Luckily, the company was a lot more successful. It was my ticket out and I took it. Whatever I did to get it was worth it.'

'Your ticket out of what?'

'Just out,' he hedged. 'It's an expression,' he added. He definitely wasn't getting into that. 'Anyway, Helen's father died two months ago and left her his shares and his seat on the board of directors. Which is why I'm in London, selling the company.'

'So you don't have to deal with Helen?' she said, making it sound like theirs had been a real marriage.

'Nothing that dramatic. I can handle Helen fine,' he said easily. 'Unfortunately she has a problem handling me. Or rather leaving me alone. And anyway, it was time to let the company go. I was going to expand anyway. I've got more control if I start afresh, with a new board of directors. New designs. My own finance. And I can cut my ties to London for good.'

'Did Helen know?'

'Did Helen know what?'

'That her father had forced you into the marriage?'

'He didn't exactly force me.' He laughed, but heard the bitterness that he thought he'd got over years ago. 'More like persuaded. There were no shotguns involved.' He stretched back against the chair, glad to have steered the conversation away from anything too revealing. 'But to answer your question, yeah, Helen knew,' he said, thinking of the lies Helen had told her father, about how Jace had taken her virginity. 'She was used to having Daddy get her what she wanted,' he continued. No need to tell Cassie exactly how stupid he'd been— and railing against all the wrongs his ex-wife had done him had never been his style. His marriage hadn't meant enough to him to make vilifying Helen all that worthwhile. 'And for some unknown reason, she wanted my ring on her finger.'

'She must have loved you,' Cassie murmured.

He swigged the cool, clear water, astonished by how sincere she sounded. Did people really believe all that rubbish? But he could see by the forthright tilt of her chin, the conviction in her eyes, that she did.

Funny that her gullibility should seem enchanting though, rather than simply naive.

He jerked his shoulder. 'Maybe.' He didn't care either way whether Helen had loved him or not.

What was a little disturbing, though, was realising that he did care what Cassie thought of him now she knew the truth.

'Eat up,' he said, nodding at Cassie's sandwich, which she'd barely touched. He stood up. 'I'll go get us some coffee, then we can grab a cab.'

He wanted to get back to the hotel…where he knew lots of good ways to avoid any more dumb conversations about his past.

Cassie picked at her sandwich and watched Jace walk away.

He stopped at the diner's retro counter, his shoulders stiff and unyielding as he spoke to the waitress. Taking her napkin out of her lap, Cassie folded it neatly over the remains of her meal as confusion made her stomach churn. What she'd learned about Jace and his marriage had killed her appetite completely.

He'd been surprisingly open, answering all her questions despite his statement on their first night that he didn't like talking about it. And now she could see why. Despite his flat, emotionless tone, and the apparent ease with which he'd told her he'd married his wife for her father's money, she couldn't help thinking that what he'd revealed raised a lot more questions than it answered.

He clearly wanted her to believe that money had been his only motivation, but she knew it was a lot more complicated than that. For despite his obvious wealth, he didn't seem like a man who was motivated by money. He didn't even like to shop, for goodness' sake. Which meant that it hadn't been the money, it had been what the money represented—the opportunity to escape—that had really been driving him. So why had he been so desperate to escape? And what had he been

so desperate to escape from? So desperate that he'd been prepared to endure a loveless marriage.

He wanted her to believe he was shallow. An opportunist.
But she knew from the other things he'd said about the web
design business that had been his ticket out that he'd worked
extremely hard to make it a success.

As a teenager, she'd conjured up lots of bad-boy fantasies
about how all he really needed was someone to love him and
support him. Someone like her. All of which had been ridiculous, and had had much more to do with her need to be
needed than anything else.

But maybe there was a grain of truth in some of it. Because
she could see now that surly disaffected boy hadn't disappeared completely.

He walked back through the tables, carrying a tray laden
with her latte and his espresso. With his shoulders slightly
hunched and his dark hair falling carelessly across his brow,
she suddenly had a vivid picture of him at seventeen, the day
he'd come into school with a vicious cut across his brow and
a black eye. Everyone had assumed he'd been in a fight.

The rush of tenderness made her stomach lighten and an
idea formed in her mind. A wonderful idea that she should
have thought of sooner.

'You didn't finish your sandwich,' he said as he placed the
coffees on the table.

'I know.' She grasped her handbag, slung it over her shoulder, then took a quick burning sip of the latte. 'I hate to eat
and run, but I have to dash. I should take this haul back to my
flat and wrap them. My best friend Nessa's doing Christmas
lunch tomorrow and everyone will be there.'

He sipped his espresso. 'All right, I'll see you at the hotel
later.' It wasn't a question, but she could see the flicker of
uncertainty in his eyes and the tenderness wrapped around
her heart, warming her more than the latte.

'You want a hand getting all that loot into a cab?' he asked as she gathered up the array of different bags, struggling to hold them all.

'I've got them. I'm an expert at this, remember.' Leaning over him, she gave him a quick kiss.

His hand settled on her waist, and he tugged her closer, turning the kiss from quick to burning in a heartbeat. 'Don't be too long,' he said when he let her go.

As she dashed off past the displays of Japanese noodles and exclusive French wine she could feel him watching her, and a wide grin spread across her face.

Jace Ryan was going to celebrate Christmas this year. Whether he had planned to or not. Because it was way past time he discovered how much he had been missing.

CHAPTER THIRTEEN

'Merry Christmas, Mr Ryan,' Cassie murmured as she settled onto Jace's lap.

His arms came around her waist and he gave her a hard hug. 'Same goes, Ms Fitzgerald.' He nuzzled her neck, and she felt her pulse leap. They'd just had a leisurely bath together and demolished a huge cooked breakfast. 'What time do you have to be at your friend's house?' he asked.

She drew back. 'Not for a while.'

'Great!' He shifted, stood up with her in his arms, but as he headed to the bedroom she wriggled down.

'Not so fast,' she said breathlessly, anticipation making her heart flutter in her chest. 'I have a surprise for you. In honour of the season.' She'd promised herself she wasn't going to make a big deal of it. But she was still looking forward to seeing his reaction.

'Oh, yeah.' He sent her a suggestive grin and grabbed the tie on her robe. 'That's what I was hoping.'

She slapped his hand away playfully. 'Not that sort of surprise. You really do have a one-track mind.'

'Hey, from the way you jumped me in the whirlpool tub this morning, I'm certainly not the only one.'

She giggled at the mock irritation in his tone as she crossed to the huge spruce tree in the corner of the suite, and the stack of presents for her friends that she'd placed beneath it yesterday evening ready for her trip to Nessa's.

Taking the brightly wrapped parcel and card perched on the top, she carried it back to him. 'Merry Christmas, Jace,' she said, presenting the gift.

Instead of taking it, he pushed his hands into the pockets of his robe, a puzzled frown creasing his brow. 'What's this?' he asked.

'It's a Christmas present,' she said brightly, holding it up. But his hands stayed buried in his pockets, the confused frown becoming more acute as he stared at the present, as if it were an unexploded bomb.

'But I told you, I don't bother with Christmas presents,' he said, his eyes lifting to hers.

She lowered the present, the flutter in her chest turning to a deep pounding beat as she registered the expression on his face. She'd expected him to be surprised. But she'd persuaded herself that the decision to buy the present was simply to thank him for giving her back that part of herself she'd lost. She had to admit now, though, that the decision had also been a little bit of a ploy to jolt him out of his cynicism about Christmas. What she hadn't expected, however, was the dazed shock in his eyes. Seemed she'd given him a bit more than a jolt.

'I didn't get you anything,' he said, his voice hoarse, his stance stiff.

'I know,' she said, emotion gripping her chest at the thought that he would be worried about that. 'I didn't expect you to.' Taking his arm, she lifted his hand out of his pocket, placed the gift in his open palm. 'It's just a token, Jace. To say thank you for everything you've given me over the last week.'

'What have I given you?' he said, the dry note of suspicion strangely defensive.

'Lots of really amazing sex,' she said lightly, but as she saw his stance relax a little she realised he'd given her so much more than that.

Being with him had been exciting and exhilarating; it had liberated her from the mistakes of her past relationships. Instead of worrying about the future, and where things were leading, with him she'd been able to stay in the moment, to enjoy their relationship for what it was with none of the weight of responsibility. And she'd had fun. More fun than she'd ever had before. Christmas had been something she'd been dreading this year, because she was going to be alone on Christmas morning, which would have reminded her a bit too forcefully of her first Christmas without her mother.

The rush of tenderness from the day before intensified. She knew she couldn't tell him any of that. Because it would alter their fling in a way neither of them wanted. But giving him the present seemed like the perfect way to say it without words.

'So thanks for that,' she added saucily. 'Plus you've been paying for all the room service, so I feel I owe you one,' she said.

He gave a rough chuckle, turned the present over in his hands as if he didn't quite know what to do with it. 'I'm not sure if I should feel used or flattered that you're giving me a gift for services rendered.'

'I'd say probably a bit of both.' She gave a light laugh, impossibly pleased that she'd got him to accept the gift. 'Why don't you open it?' she prompted.

He looked up. 'All right.' He sat back down in his chair, then eased off the sticky tape with such care her heart began to hammer her ribcage. It was almost as if he'd never received a gift before. Which was ridiculous, but somehow she couldn't shake the thought as he lifted the emerald-green designer sweater she'd bought the day before and held it up as if it were incredibly precious. The colour matched his eyes and the cashmere was soft enough that it wouldn't irritate his skin if he chose to wear it without a T-shirt.

'Cassie, this is expensive. Too expensive.'

'Do you like it?' she asked, although she didn't need to, she could see the astonished wonder in his face, which she suspected had as much to do with getting the gift as it did with the gift itself.

'You know I do. But I can't—'

'It wasn't that expensive,' she interrupted. 'It certainly didn't cost as much as four days' worth of room-service meals at The Chesterton.' She lifted the card off the table, handed it to him. 'You forgot the card.'

Her pulse sped up as he took it, shaking his head. 'You shouldn't have gone to all this trouble.'

She smiled, glad that she had. Suddenly struck by the realisation that despite his success, and his money and his industrial strength sex appeal, Jace Ryan had never made any meaningful human connections in his life. Not with his so-called friends, not during his short-lived marriage and certainly not with his family... Or he wouldn't have been so completely poleaxed by a simple Christmas gift. As a teenager, she'd always believed in her typically rose-tinted way that what he needed was true love, but maybe all he had really needed was a friend. A proper friend. And she could be that. At least for the short time they were together.

Jace drew the white card out of the envelope and stared at the picture on it while willing the tightening in his chest to go the hell away.

But it didn't go away, it got worse as he studied the expertly drawn caricature of himself standing next to a Christmas tree with piles of shopping bags under it, his bare chest looking like something out of a body-builders magazine while the seductive smile on his face was tinged with wickedness. The words written underneath in an elaborate serif font read:

To Jace, Ex-Bad Boy, Candy Man extraordinaire and Champion Shopper in training!
Merry Christmas, Cassidy x

He huffed out a laugh past the constriction in his throat, so touched by the silly card he felt like an idiot. Who knew the Christmas spirit could be contagious?

He looked up to find her watching him, her face flushed with pleasure. Dropping the card on the table, he shifted round and grasped the tie on her robe. 'Come here, clever clogs,' he said, dragging her towards him until she straddled his lap. She rested her hands on his shoulders, the sweet, impossibly pleased smile on her face making his insides flip over—a strange feeling of lightness and excitement and anticipation swelling right alongside the lust.

'I feel kind of bad,' he said, stroking his thumb across her collarbone, and watching her pulse flutter against her neck, 'that I don't have anything for you in return.'

'That's okay, Jace.' Her eyes went to half mast as his index finger traced the line of her throat then dipped down to explore the tempting display of cleavage revealed by the lapels of her robe. 'Don't you know, it's much better to give than to receive?' she purred, her voice husky with desire.

'Is that so?' He nudged aside her robe, heard the sharp intake of breath as he exposed the fullness of her breast and the swollen nipple to his gaze. 'Then I guess it's my turn to do the giving,' he said before swirling his tongue across the puckered flesh and drawing it into his mouth.

She bucked in his lap, her fingers digging into his shoulders as he feasted on her. But as the blood pounded into his groin, the lump in his throat swelled and he had to push down the tidal wave of regret that he would never be able to give her more than this.

'I shouldn't be here,' Jace grumbled as Cassie stabbed the doorbell on the wall panel for the red-brick block of flats situated next to the shutters of a closed shop. The metal frames of the market stalls stood behind them, making the empty Hoxton Street Market look eerily quiet in the cold afternoon air. 'I wasn't invited.'

'Nessa won't mind,' Cassie replied, glancing over her shoulder, her cheeks pink from the cold. 'Why would she?'

'Because she doesn't know me,' he said, stating the blatantly obvious. And more to the point, he didn't know her.

He still wasn't quite sure how he'd got strong-armed into coming to Cassie's friend's Christmas meal in the first place. One minute he'd been riding on the crest of a wave of endorphins, the heady rush of afterglow tempered by the confusing emotions Cassie had caused by giving him the Christmas gift. And the next he'd been driving through the deserted streets of East London en route to a dinner date with a load of strangers.

He'd had a perfectly good plan to go jogging in Hyde Park, sweat off the room-service meals he'd been devouring in the hotel and then catch up on reading through some of the proposals his PA had emailed him from the various buyers he still hadn't got round to meeting.

He didn't want to be here. So why was he?

'Of course Nessa knows you,' Cassie said matter-of-factly, giving the door a hefty shove when it buzzed. 'She went to Hillsdown Road too.'

'Terrific,' he muttered sarcastically, tension tightening his shoulder blades as he held the door open for Cassie and her sack full of gifts.

'Don't look so worried.' She grinned, patting his cheek. 'You were a legend at Hillsroad.'

'Which is exactly what I'm worried about,' he said grimly as he trudged up the darkened stairwell behind her.

The door on the first-floor landing was painted a glaring shade of yellow with black and green edging. And the pulsing beat of a current funk rap anthem could be heard from inside.

Jace braced himself as the door swung open and a curvaceous black woman wearing a beaded tunic, similar to the one Cassie had had on that first night, came bounding out and flung her arms round Cassie. 'Hey, girl? What's up?'

Cassie dropped the bags and hugged her friend back. 'Happy Chrimbo, Ness. I hope you've got enough turkey for one more?' She stood back, and the woman's lushly made-up eyes landed on Jace.

'Oh, my days, Jace the Ace!' she proclaimed.

Jace winced. He'd never liked that nickname much at school, he was liking it even less now.

'Haven't you grown up nice?' she said and then sent him a cheeky grin that had memory blindsiding him.

He grinned back. 'Damn, Vanessa Douglas,' he said, his shoulders relaxing for the first time since he'd agreed to come. 'The scourge of the lower third.'

She laughed, the sound rich and full, and he recalled how much he'd enjoyed it when they'd ended up in detention together—which with her smart mouth and his aptitude for trouble had been fairly frequently.

'Guilty as charged,' she said, giving him a high five. 'Remember how we made Ms Clavell's life a living hell?'

'The poor woman nearly had a breakdown,' Jace said, amazed to realise he'd now discovered two memories from school that hadn't been at all bad.

'That woman was way too uptight.' Nessa batted the

thought away as she shut the door behind them. 'We just loosened her up a bit.'

She turned to Cassie as they followed her into the flat's cramped hallway and took off their coats. 'And of course I've got enough turkey. The thing's a mutant,' she added, hanging up their coats as the scents of roasting meat and Caribbean spices wafted down the hallway, along with the shouts of raucous conversation and the bass-heavy music. 'Terrence had to cut the legs off to fit it in the oven,' she said, leading them into a surprisingly large open-plan kitchen-diner, which was packed with people who were chatting and chopping and cooking and carousing in that disorderly but choreographed way that old friends did instinctively.

Clapping her hands, Nessa got everyone's attention.

A tall, good-looking, mixed-race guy standing by the stove with an apron on that said 'World's sexiest chef' turned down the speakers on the counter top.

'Okay, folks, Cassie's here and she's brought her new candy man, Jace. So treat him nice.'

Cassie slapped Nessa's arm, blushing profusely as she hissed over the chorus of cheers and wolf whistles from her friends, 'Ness, I can't believe you just said that.'

Jace choked out a laugh, the last of the tension easing out of his shoulders as he got slapped on the back by one of the guys and offered a hearty handshake by another.

So, Vanessa Douglas still had the smartest mouth in London.

'I reckon you've finally found yourself a keeper.'

Cassie glanced over her shoulder, her arms elbow deep in soapy water, the noise from the raucous game of Twister in the living room covering Nessa's murmured comment. The heat hit her neck as she gave what she hoped was a nonchalant shrug.

'You mean Jace?'

'Mmm-hmm.' Nessa slanted her a don't-play-the-innocent-with-me look. 'So what happened to "I'm not ready for too much spectacular sex"?' she teased in a little-girl voice.

Cassie coughed out a laugh and put the washed saucepan on the draining board. 'For goodness' sake, Ness, keep your voice down. After that candy-man comment everyone's going to think I'm a loose woman.'

'Like it isn't already obvious how loose you are,' Nessa said, picking up a tea towel.

Cassie's blush intensified, but her lips quirked at Nessa's typically saucy observation.

She'd had such a good time this afternoon, it was hard to get snippy with her best mate for pointing out the obvious. And in a funny way, the fact that Nessa could tell what a difference her days with Jace had made to her state of well-being reinforced her decision to indulge in her wild fling.

The afternoon had gone better than she could have hoped. And that had been mostly down to Jace. While it had taken a lot of persuasion and quite a bit of trickery to get him to Nessa's, he'd relaxed and enjoyed himself once he was here. Her friends were a close-knit group, having all known each other since they were teenagers, but with his sharp wit and easy-going charm Jace had fitted right in. He'd joined in with their banter, told some entertaining stories about life in New York, wowed everyone with the apps on his phone that were just a small segment of his company's output and had bonded with Nessa's fiancé, Terrence, over the subject of Spurs' chances of making Europe this year.

Funny to think that even after three years of dating Lance, none of her friends had ever hit it off with him nearly as well.

'So what's happening with you two?' Nessa asked, picking up the wet saucepan. 'Seems like you've got off to an excellent start.'

Cassie deposited a frying pan on the sideboard, and quashed the silly pang radiating up her torso. 'It's not the start of anything. It's nothing more than a Christmas fling. He's going back to New York on New Year's Day and that'll be the end of it.'

Nessa shoved the saucepan in a cupboard with a loud clatter. 'That's stupid. Why don't you go over to New York with him for a while? See how things work out? You can draw anywhere.'

'Ness, stop being absurd. Quite apart from the fact that he hasn't invited me.' And he wasn't likely to, she thought as the silly pang got worse. 'I told you, this isn't a relationship. It's just a bit of fun.' Which was all she wanted, she told herself staunchly. But her golden glow from the afternoon faded a little.

'Uh-huh,' Nessa said, scepticism oozing from every pore. 'You wanna know what I think?'

Cassie yanked the plug out and wiped her hands on Nessa's tea towel. 'Not really, but I'm sure you're going to tell me anyway.'

'He can't take his eyes off you, especially when he thinks you aren't looking. And your gaze follows him wherever he goes too. And you buy him a sweater that he wears first chance he gets. Plus you've been having spectacular sex for the last four days without an intermission.' Nessa doggedly counted off the points on her fingers, then slapped her hands on her hips. 'That *is* the start of something. It's the start of something called a relationship.'

Cassie blew out a careful breath, tried to quell the seed of hope that had been budding inside her all day. The seed of hope that wanted to believe that what Nessa was saying was true, when her head already knew it wasn't. 'It's not a relationship. It only looks that way.'

Nessa made a scoffing sound. 'Why do you always sell yourself short like that?'

'I'm not, I'm being realistic.'

Nessa waved the comment away with a flick of her wrist. 'So that's what they call giving up now, is it? Realism.'

'I'm not giving up, it's not like that.' She couldn't let herself hope again. Hope for something that wasn't real. She'd learned that lesson too often to want to learn it again. And worse, she somehow knew that if she let herself dream for something permanent with Jace, the devastation would be that much worse. Because he already meant more to her—in four scant days—than Lance had meant to her after three years. 'You've never had anyone tell you to your face, in the most graphic way possible, that you didn't matter, so you don't know what it's like,' she hit back.

'Maybe not,' Nessa conceded. 'But then I never made the mistake of hitching my dreams to guys that weren't worth the effort either.'

'What's that supposed to mean?' Cassie whispered, shocked by the accusation in her friend's voice. Nessa had been the Rock of Gibraltar throughout her adolescence and her adult life. She was the one who had always been there, picking her up when the men in her life had let her down, or abandoned her, or cheated on her.

Nessa gripped her upper arms, gave her a little shake. 'Don't get all pinched face on me. I'm not saying what Lance did was your fault. You're the one who said that. But what I am saying is why did you ever settle for someone like him in the first place? He was never good enough for you, honey, but you were the only one who couldn't see it. Now you're falling in love with Jace Ryan, a guy who might actually be worthy of you, and you're too scared to even admit it 'cos for some dumb reason you think you're not entitled to be that happy.'

'It's not that...' Her voice trailed off. She wasn't falling in love with Jace; she couldn't be. Her panic button wasn't just tripping now—alarm bells were blaring out at full blast.

'Stop freaking out,' Nessa said, pulling her into a hard hug. 'All I'm saying is, if you decide you want him, don't be scared to fight for him.' She drew back, held Cassie at arm's length, a confident smile spreading across her lips. 'Because it's exactly like they say in that hair ad. You're worth it, honey.'

CHAPTER FOURTEEN

'WHO's Lance?' Jace shifted gears too forcefully, making the rental car's engine whine.

'Hmm?' Cassie glanced over from the passenger seat. She'd been subdued since they'd left Nessa's place. But then so had he.

He'd had a good time. The food had been fabulous, and plentiful, and the company even better. But there was something about seeing Cassie with her friends, and getting drawn into their Christmas celebration, that had been kind of unsettling towards the end of the evening. As they'd said their goodbyes, it had occurred to him that he'd never see these people again. And for the first time ever he actually regretted the transient nature of the friendships in his own life.

Not that he was missing anything, he reassured himself. He had friends. Just not people he wanted to depend on, the way Cassie clearly depended on hers. But watching the way she blossomed in their company had been captivating. Gone was the woman who seemed unsure of herself. She had been more confident, more in control—just as she was when they made love.

Or at least she had been, until Terrence had made a passing reference to this guy Lance. Cassie had changed the subject and, after a few knowing looks had passed between her friends, they'd gone along with it. It was obvious they all felt protective towards her. Which had made him wonder what exactly it was they were protecting her from. Then of course he'd had to wonder why he cared.

But even knowing he shouldn't care who Lance was, he hadn't been able to stop the question spilling out.

It was just curiosity. He wanted to know why she'd changed the subject, and why the mention of the guy's name had caused that moment of distress to flash across her face.

'Or Lance the Loser, to give him his full name,' Jace prompted, jerking his gaze from the road to watch her reaction.

A frown line appeared on her brow. 'He's nobody,' she said. 'Not any more.'

His fingers fisted on the steering wheel. So he did have something to do with Cassie. 'But he was someone once,' he said. 'So who was he?'

And what was he to you?

She sighed, turned to look back out of the window as the darkened shops along Kingsland High Road whipped past. 'We were engaged to be married,' she murmured. 'Until I found him doing the bare-butt boogie on my sofa with one of his ex-girlfriends.' She huffed out a little laugh, but there was no humour in it. 'I should have dumped him for being such a cliché, even without the cheating.'

'Is he the relationship that came to a bad end?' he asked, unable to keep the edge out of his voice as his knuckles whitened.

Loser was right. What kind of lowlife did that to a woman? Especially a woman as sweet-natured and generous as Cassie?

'Yes, that would be Lance.' Her affirmation sounded resigned and touched something deep inside him that hadn't been touched in longer than he could remember.

The urge to comfort and reassure came from nowhere.

Reaching across the console, he put his hand on her leg, squeezed. 'He was obviously a total jerk.'

'I know.' She sighed heavily. 'My problem is that I seem to be a magnet for total jerks. Even my dad was a total jerk.'

'Yeah, how's that?' he asked, not sure he really wanted to know the answer. He knew what it was like to be screwed up by a parent. Thinking of Cassie having to go through that wasn't the best way to keep his anger under control.

'He didn't do anything that terrible,' she said carefully. 'I've always been oversensitive about it.'

He doubted that, given the way she'd let Lance the Loser off the hook. 'What did your father do?'

'It's not what he did. It's what he didn't do.'

He waited for her to elaborate.

'My parents got divorced when I was four,' she began. 'He'd found someone else, and started a new family with her. He hurt my mum terribly but she maintained contact with him because she wanted me to have a relationship with him. Only problem was, I don't think he was ever that interested. He felt guilty and obligated, so he went through the motions.' She gave a soft sigh and he felt the pulse of anger beat in his temple.

He'd never considered becoming a father because he knew he wouldn't be any good at it. His own role models had been atrocious and he didn't like to rely on anyone, or have them rely on him. But even he couldn't imagine being uninterested in your own flesh and blood.

'He'd say he was going to take me to do this and that,' Cassie murmured, her voice so quiet he almost couldn't hear it. 'We'd make arrangements, I'd get all excited and then...' She paused. 'Mostly, he didn't show. He'd ring at the last minute with some excuse. And the few times he did show, usually because my mum had pressured him into it, he'd be preoccupied, talking on his mobile, or getting irritated with me if I asked too many questions. He was a busy man and he let me know that he didn't have time for me.'

'Good thing he didn't show up more often,' Jace said forcefully, thinking what a waste of space the guy must have been.

'What?'

He shrugged. 'Sounds like you were well rid of him. Who wants to spend time with a jerk like that.'

'Do you know something? I've never even thought of it like that.' She laughed, but this time the sound had the light tinkle of real amusement. 'But you're right. Whenever he didn't turn up, my mum would take me out instead. We'd go ice-skating or swimming, or one time she took me and Ness to the Open Air Theatre in Regent's Park and we had a great time. She was always more fun than him anyway.'

The genuine pleasure in her voice had the uneasiness prickling up his spine again.

'There you go,' he murmured, lifting his hand off her knee. *Time to back off. You don't get involved, remember?*

'What were your parents like, Jace?' she asked softly.

He flinched. Where had that question come from?

He flipped up the indicator, then gripped the gear shift as he accelerated past St Paul's Cathedral, the silence in the car suddenly deafening.

Cassie listened to the quiet hum of the powerful car's engine and watched Jace's jaw tense.

'Why do you ask?' he said, so evasively her heart pummelled her chest. She should probably let the subject drop, but his defensiveness was so unlike the confident man she had come to know, she didn't want to back down. Had his parents been the thing he had wanted to escape?

'When we were at school, I overheard Ms Tremall saying you came from a bad home,' she said. 'I always wondered what on earth she meant.'

'I guess she meant it wasn't good.' He laughed, the sound brittle. 'But it wasn't that terrible. And it's so long ago now, it doesn't matter.'

Why did she have the feeling it did matter, then? She thought of the unguarded look of surprise and pleasure on his face when he had unwrapped her gift that morning, and realised it mattered a lot.

'How bad was it?'

He looked at her as the car braked at the traffic lights along Fleet Street, his expression carefully blank. The sound of his thumb tapping a rapid tattoo on the steering wheel cut through the evening quiet. 'You know what?' he began, his voice tense. 'How about we skip this conversation?'

Cassie studied the stiff set of his shoulders as he pressed his foot to the accelerator. 'Why do you want to skip it, if it doesn't matter?'

He accelerated as the lights changed, and hitched his shoulders. 'Okay, fine,' he said, his voice clipped. 'If you really want to know, my mum married a guy when I was eight who had a violent temper and didn't make much of an effort to control it.'

Cassie's stomach tensed, the faded scar across his left eyebrow illuminated by the lights of Charing Cross Station. 'He *hit* you?'

'Not too much. I got very good at staying out of his way. And eventually I got big enough to fight back,' he replied, in a tense monotone. 'My mum took the worst of it.'

'Jace,' she whispered, covering the hand he had wrapped around the gear shift. 'I'm so sorry.' Tears pricked the backs of her eyelids at the thought of what he must have witnessed and endured. 'That's hideous.'

He stared at her briefly in the half-light. 'There's nothing to be sorry about. I'm all grown up now and it's over.'

He pulled his hand out from under hers, rested his palm on her knee.

'How about we change the subject—' his hand trailed up her leg '—and concentrate on something a lot more interesting?'

She forced a weak smile to her lips, swallowed the tears down, as the familiar rush of heat sizzled up her thigh where his hand wandered. 'Okay, Mr One-Track Mind,' she joked, trying not to let her wayward emotions overwhelm her.

But as they drove round Trafalgar Square the light flurries of snow framed the giant Norwegian Spruce at its centre and made the view from her window as the car sped past look as picturesque and magical as a Christmas card. Her heart thundered and her mind raced, unable to let go of the image of Jace as a boy and the miserable home life that had been exactly the opposite of a Christmas card.

He didn't need a friend. He needed so much more than that. Something she knew in her heart she could give him. As soon as the thought registered she tried to push it down and bury it deep. But it was already too late.

She turned to look at the man next to her as he negotiated the steady stream of traffic on Piccadilly Circus. She considered the harsh line of his jaw, the dark concentration on his brow and the closed expression on his handsome face that gave so little away even when they were making love—then pushed out a ragged breath.

Nessa was right. She *was* falling for Jace. Or why would she have been so devastated by that brief insight into the horrors he'd suffered as a child? And why would she believe she could fix it?

She pushed her head into the deep bucket seat, listened to the purr of the powerful car and struggled to calm her heart's frantic leaps and pirouettes.

So she was falling for Jace. But what the hell did she do about it?

Should she tell him? Or would that complicate things even more?

'That's it, Cassie. Come for me again,' Jace rasped, sweat popping on his brow, the corded muscles in his arms and neck straining as her hot slick flesh tightened around him. He drove deep, clung onto sanity, the exquisite torture pushing him to the brink. Her eyes glazed over, her body bowed back and the ragged sobs of fulfilment echoed in his ear as he crashed over right behind her.

He drew out slowly, the dull ache in his groin from the intensity of his climax nothing compared to the raw rush of emotion clutching at his chest as she gazed up at him.

Her palm cupped his cheek, her eyes alight with an emotion so pure and elemental a muscle in his jaw clenched. As always her expression was as open and easy to read as a children's picture book.

Don't say it, Cassie.

He placed a kiss on her lips before she could speak. 'That was terrific,' he said, keeping his voice deliberately flippant. 'Merry Christmas, Cassie.'

Shifting off her, he slung his arm round her shoulders, tucked her against his side and braced himself to hear the words he feared she was about to say.

She wouldn't be the first woman to tell him she loved him. He'd seen that look in a woman's eyes dozens of times before. Women often got sentimental after great sex and—after his momentary lapse in the car when he'd told her about his stepfather, and the dumb way he'd reacted to her present, plus the fact that he and Cassie had been having great sex for nearly a week—it was kind of inevitable that someone as romantic as Cassie would fall into the familiar trap. What did surprise him, though, was that he hadn't seen it coming, and he didn't know what the hell he was going to do about it.

She was the first woman he'd ever been scared to hear say it. Because for the first time ever, he knew the usual ploys he used to deal with the dreaded 'I love you' moment wouldn't work.

He couldn't lie, as he usually did. Just repeat the phrase as casually as possible, or simply brush it off and then forget about it. Because Cassie would see right through it. And if he told her the truth, that as far as he was concerned love was just a gimmick that people used to trap each other, she'd be hurt. And he didn't want to hurt her. Not only that, but she might walk out on him. And while he knew it was selfish of him—not to mention arrogant and egotistical—he didn't want her to walk. Not yet. She was good company, she was sexy as hell, and he liked the way she looked at him—with that strange combination of innocence and confidence and understanding. It made him feel lighter, more optimistic than he had in a long time. As if all the mistakes he'd made in his life, all the things he'd done wrong, didn't matter if he was with her.

'Merry Christmas, Jace,' she whispered at last.

Relief washed through him, the lucky escape making him feel like a man who'd just walked away from a firing squad.

She hadn't said it. Thank God.

He frowned. Had he just imagined that look?

The frown deepened. Okay, too much great sex was clearly making him a little nutty too because why should that bother him? This was good news.

He skimmed his hand down her back, felt her lush body curl against him—and shoved down the stupid swell of contentment that followed.

'How about we get out of here tomorrow?' he suggested. 'Go someplace?' There were tons of things they could do in

London. They'd hardly been out of the hotel suite and—while he was going to find it torture keeping his hands off her—he probably needed to reduce the physical intensity for a while. And after Boxing Day he really needed to get stuck into those meetings that he'd been holding off on too.

Today had got way too intense, for a number of reasons. Letting her simple Christmas gift get to him had been bad enough, but then blurting out all that stuff about his childhood and letting the sympathy and compassion shining in her eyes get to him too had only compounded the problem. Cassie had slipped under his guard somehow, and it was a mistake he would have to correct, and fast. They only had six more days before his flight back to New York and by then he was letting her go.

She lifted up, propped her elbows on his chest to look down at him, her full breasts distracting him as they swayed enticingly.

'Mr One-Track Mind isn't seriously suggesting we do something other than sex, is he?'

He choked out a laugh, then grasped her hips and neatly reversed their positions, nestling his hardening erection against her stomach.

'Don't push your luck, Cassidy. Or you may find yourself imprisoned here for another six days.'

Much later, after the storm of passion had passed a second time, Cassie lay awake listening to the steady rise and fall of Jace's breathing and blinked back the foolish tears.

She'd nearly blurted out the words. Nearly declared her feelings earlier. But then she'd seen him flinch, almost as if he knew what she was about to say, and she'd managed to hold back, the frigid chill settling in the pit of her belly.

Just because her heart went out to the boy Jace had once been and she was tumbling into love with the man he had managed to become. Just because she had convinced herself that his life could be richer with her in it, and vice versa, she had to remember that Jace had never asked her for a thing.

And until he did, until he gave her some sign that his feelings had deepened too, she'd be mad to tell him how she felt and risk ruining what little time they had left.

CHAPTER FIFTEEN

'It's time for some candy floss,' Jace announced, gripping Cassie's gloved hand and hauling her through the milling crowd towards the confectionery stand.

'No more food, I'm begging you,' Cassie groaned comically, rubbing her belly. 'We had hot dogs half an hour ago. And my stomach's still in revolt after the Big Dipper.'

'See, I prove my point.' Jace laughed, stopping at the stand. 'Women make rubbish dates at funfairs.'

He ordered a large helping of candy floss from the vendor.

'That is such a load of crap.' Cassie slapped her hands on her hips in mock outrage as he took a huge bite of the giant helping of spun sugar. 'I had my brain scrambled on the Twister, took the Helter Skelter at close to sixty miles per hour and nearly swallowed my own tongue on the Power Tower,' she declared, still shuddering at the memory of plunging a hundred and fifty feet in free fall. 'And I didn't make a single complaint.'

He wrapped one arm around her hips, yanked her close and gave her a sugar-coated kiss. His devastating green eyes twinkled with humour. 'You screamed like a girl in the Haunted House.'

A smile edged her lips, the bud of hope that had been building for days blossoming in her chest at the affection on his face. 'A severed head flew past my ear,' she muttered, trying to sound stern. 'I should get a pass on that.'

He touched his nose to hers, the cold tip sending little shivers of excitement down her spine as the smell of burnt sugar and man engulfed her. 'You didn't hear *me* screaming, did you?' he murmured, his low voice intimate and amused.

She shoved him back, laughing. 'You definitely flinched.'

'A manly flinch is permitted. My ears are still ringing from that scream.'

She cocked her eyebrow. 'So now who's complaining?'

Taking her hand, his fingers closed around hers as he chuckled. 'Not me,' he said. 'I guess you make a pretty good funfair date,' he added magnanimously, swinging their joined hands as they strolled through the thoroughfare of Christmas-themed market stalls at the entrance to the funfair that was set up every year in Hyde Park. 'For a girl,' he finished.

She socked him on the arm, making him laugh. Then shuddered as the brittle winter wind found its way through the bare chestnut trees sheltering the fair and whipped at her hair.

He slung his arm over her shoulder, hugged her against his side as he dumped the last of the candy floss in a rubbish bin. 'How about we head back to the hotel? Get you warmed up.'

She circled his lean waist, leant against him as they strolled out of the park together. But she knew she didn't need warming up, the spark inside her that had ignited days ago now burning like a log fire and giving her a golden glow inside and out.

The last five days had been magical. He'd handled all his business meetings with ruthless efficiency first thing in the mornings, leaving the afternoons and evenings free to play. And play they had.

They'd gone ice-skating at the crowded rink in front of the Natural History Museum. Feasted on fine French wine

and steak and *pomme frites* in the stark Mayfair elegance
of Quaglino's and on champagne and oysters in the Italian
gothic splendour of Bentley's Bar and Grill in Piccadilly.
They'd taken long walks with his arm around her shoulders
through the frost-bitten parklands of Kensington Gardens.
And she'd even managed to drag him to the Boxing Day
sales along Oxford Street where he'd endured over an hour
of bargain hunting before he'd made her spend almost as long
genuflecting over the newest gizmos in the gadget store on
Regent Street.

And every night they'd made passionate love in the seclu-
sion of his penthouse suite. Her senses and physical awareness
of him were so acute now, all he had to do was look at her
with hunger burning in his eyes and she became moist, her
body readying itself to indulge in all the pleasure she knew
he was about to give her.

She was falling in love and she wasn't scared of her feelings any more.

They hadn't had any more conversations about serious
stuff, like her past or his. They hadn't discussed what would
happen in two days' time when he returned to New York.
And he hadn't said anything specific to her about continuing
their affair. But sometimes actions spoke louder than words.
The appreciation and affection and approval that shone in
his emerald gaze whenever he looked at her. The way he
couldn't stop touching her: the hand-holding, the fleeting
kisses, the impromptu hugs, the palm brushes down her hair
or the knuckles he skimmed across her cheek whenever they
were in public. And then there was the way he made love to
her, sometimes two or three times a night and often in the
morning too, with a power and a passion and an urgency that
increased in its intensity with each passing day.

All those things could only mean one thing.

Jace was falling for her too. Although she suspected, given his past relationships with women, he didn't have a clue.

Tomorrow was New Year's Eve and he'd arranged for them to watch the countdown and the fireworks from the balcony of an exclusive nightclub overlooking the Thames.

As his arm tightened around her shoulders, and the garish sights and sounds of the winter funfair faded, she made her own special New Year's resolution. If he didn't say anything by tomorrow night, she would take the initiative.

Nessa had told her she should fight for what she wanted. And she intended to do just that.

She wasn't going to put undue pressure on him and make some lavish declaration of undying love. But why shouldn't she see if they had a future together? It seemed foolish to let what they had slip away, just because both of them were too scared, or too cautious or too clueless about love to admit their feelings for one another went deeper than a Christmas fling.

'Only ten minutes to go, then we can make our getaway,' Jace murmured against Cassie's hair as his hands skimmed over her waist.

He heard her draw in a quick breath, his palms settling on the cool silk covering her hips.

'I don't think so,' she whispered, her eyes connecting with his in the floor-to-ceiling window that looked out over the Thames. The Millennium Wheel stood proud and glaringly modern, spotlit across the choppy water as the anticipation of the well-off crowd rose with each incremental movement on Big Ben's clockface to the right of the terrace. Cassie's lips edged up in a nervous smile. 'We have to see the fireworks. The view from here is incredible.'

'I've got a much better view.' He nuzzled her ear lobe as

he caressed the sensuous silk. 'And I've got some much better fireworks in mind too.'

She giggled, covering his hands with hers, to halt his increasingly insistent caresses. 'Stop it. You didn't pay five hundred pounds a ticket to miss the main event.'

He chuckled. 'Cassidy, as far as I'm concerned, tonight's main event does not involve us being cooped up on a terrace with a hundred other people.'

She turned in his arms, lifted her hands around his neck and sent him a saucy smile. 'Well, you'll just have to be patient. This is our last night together and I want it to be special.'

He tensed slightly, his hands settling on the small of her back. She'd given him the opening he'd been waiting for. He'd been thinking about his options for days, made the final decision that morning. But now he had the chance to say the words he found himself hesitating. Evaluating the situation and the best way to handle it—and her—one last time.

Everything had worked out perfectly in the last few days. He'd had more fun in her company than he could ever remember having with another person. She seemed to understand him in ways no other woman ever had. She was bright, lively and sweetly optimistic and had no need to cling to him. In fact, her lack of expectation had made it possible for him to relax and enjoy himself without fear of having to deal with the suffocating prospect of commitment. Maybe the plan to reduce the physical intensity hadn't quite worked out, given that the instant, insistent need had turned to a constant, growing ache that he had found harder and harder to control. But he wasn't too worried about that any more. Because the 'I love you moment' he'd been dreading hadn't materialised. He'd kept things light and non-committal—even forcing himself to take time out every morning to handle the meetings his PA had rescheduled—and Cassie had gone along with it. She hadn't made any demands, or any requests even. And while part of him had been relieved, as the time drew close for him to leave he'd actually begun to find it a little galling.

Because now he was the one who was going to have to do the asking. But as she looked at him expectantly, her eyes shining with excitement, the compelling look of acceptance on her face, he knew he couldn't hold back any longer.

'About this being our last night.' He paused. 'I was thinking…' His voice trailed off.

Come on, Ryan, spit it out. It's not that big of a deal. If she says no, it won't be the end of the world.

'How busy are you right now, workwise?'

She tilted her head to one side, the shine positively glowing now. 'Why do you ask?'

His hands rode up her sides, tightened. Maybe it wouldn't be the end of the world, but the desire to hear her say yes was still pretty damn acute.

'Why don't you come back with me tomorrow?' he said, as casually as he possibly could. 'For a few days? Or a week. Or even two. I've narrowed down a buyer for the business. I'm planning to finalise the sale tomorrow. So I figured I'd take a break from work when I get home. I can show you around New York. It's an incredible city.'

He clamped his mouth shut, realising with horror he was starting to babble.

For God's sake, shut up, you sound like a boy asking a girl on a first date.

But then a huge smile spread across her face, and the panicked ticks of his heartbeat calmed.

'That's…' she began. 'I don't know what…'

'Don't say anything yet.' He pressed his lips to hers as the noise of the crowd, shouting down the final seconds of the old year, rose to a crescendo outside on the terrace. 'We've got all night for you to make a decision,' he finished.

Taking her hands from around his neck, he turned her back to face the scene outside, folded his arms over her midriff and pulled her slim body back against his. 'Now watch the fireworks.' He bit softly into her ear lobe, heard her breath catch. 'Before I drag you out of here to have my way with you.'

As the crowd roared and cheered Big Ben chimed the hour and a blast of light and colour exploded across the Thames. Cassie tilted her head back against his shoulder, looked up into his face. 'Happy New Year, Jace.'

'Yeah,' he growled, seeing the answer in her eyes. She was going to come with him.

Slanting his lips across hers, he captured her mouth in a harsh, possessive kiss, his heart thumping against his ribs and his arms tightening around her instinctively.

It was going to be a Happy New Year all right. At least for him.

He didn't have to let her go. Not just yet.

CHAPTER SIXTEEN

'So, Cassidy, it's make your mind up time.' Jace tugged her into his lap. Securing his arms round her waist to hold her in place, he asked, 'You want me to book you a ticket to the Big Apple today?'

Cassie's heart leapt into her throat, the sexy smile and the warm weight of his arms making the high she'd been riding since his offer the night before shoot straight into the stratosphere. She swallowed heavily to control the lump of emotion in her throat, ready at last to bare the feelings she had for him.

He wanted to continue their affair; she could see he cared a great deal for her—the way he'd made love to her last night when they'd arrived home from the New Year's celebrations, fast and frantic the first time, then slow and tender the next, was yet more proof of his growing feelings. But she couldn't accept his offer under false pretences. He'd been deliberately casual about how long she would be in New York and about why he wanted her there, she suspected as a defence. He was a man who had never been in love before—not even with the woman he had married—and, from the little she knew of his past and his character, had tried very hard to protect himself from any emotion likely to make him vulnerable.

But if she accepted his offer, she had to let him know that her feelings were not casual. She needed to be honest now, and go with her instinct, that his feelings weren't as casual as he tried to pretend.

Looping her arms round his neck, she gave him a soft smile, her gaze drifting over his harsh, handsome features. The dimple in his cheek, the confidence in his eyes, the locks of unruly hair still glistening from their morning tryst in the shower. She wanted to memorise every aspect of his expression when she told him she was falling in love.

'I want to come. More than anything I've ever—'

'Excellent,' he said, interrupting her. 'I'll give my PA the news. We'll need your passport number.'

He tried to shift her off his lap. She had to cling on. 'I'm not finished, Jace.'

'We need to get the ball rolling,' he said, the flash of impatience in his eye making her hesitate. 'Tickets have to be booked, bags packed and—'

'Jace, stop it. I've got something I want to tell you.'

His shoulders stiffened slightly under her hands. 'Okay, but make it quick.'

'I... If I come to New York... You need to know that I...' She stumbled, her confidence ebbing away. Why did he look so tense all of a sudden? 'This means a lot to me. Because...' She had to force the words out past lips that had dried like parchment. 'I'm falling in love with you.'

His eyebrows rose a fraction, and for a split second she thought she saw something in his face. But it was masked instantly, leaving the precious words hanging in the air between them, sounding foolish and a little corny instead of heartfelt and genuine.

'I'm flattered,' he said, the tone of his voice so condescending she cringed. 'But we've really got to get a move on if we're not going to miss our flight.' Taking her weight, he lifted her off his lap.

She folded her arms round her waist, her insides churning

as the hope and excitement of moments ago turned to bewilderment.

Placing a quick kiss on her nose, he patted her behind. 'Now go and get dressed. I'll drive you round to your place so you can pack after I've called my PA to confirm about the ticket.'

'Jace, wait.' She grasped his arm as he tried to walk past. 'Don't you have anything else to say?'

She'd expected surprise, maybe even shock, had been prepared for him to try to deny her feelings to protect the wall he had kept around his own for so long. What she hadn't expected, or even considered, was his indifference.

He shrugged. 'No,' he said.

She frowned, the tears swelling in her throat making her feel even more foolish. Was she overreacting, being stupidly sentimental? 'I just told you I'm falling in love with you,' she said carefully. She bit down on her quivering lip, knowing that tears would only make this situation a billion times more humiliating. 'Are you sure you don't have anything else to say about it?'

'I told you, I'm flattered,' he said, stressing each syllable. 'I'm glad you like me so much.' But he didn't sound glad, he sounded irritated. She could read him fairly well now, despite the way he always fought to keep his emotions hidden. She could see the slight tension in his jaw, the muscle in his cheek that flexed as he spoke. 'It'll make things more fun when we hit New York,' he finished.

Fun!

The single word sparked something deep inside her. Something that she didn't properly recognise, because she had never let it loose before. Not when her father had left her sitting on the sofa for hours with her best dress on and her hair carefully braided waiting for nothing; not when David had told her in a polite monotone he thought things weren't working out between them; not even when Lance had leapt up from the sofa, his trousers round his ankles, and demanded to know what she thought she was doing walking into her own flat without knocking.

Jace took her arm, steering her towards the bedroom. 'We can talk about this later.'

The curt words had the unfamiliar emotion burning up her torso, searing her throat and exploding through the top of her head.

'Now go and—' he continued, but the ringing in her ears got so loud it cut off the rest of the sentence.

'No, we can't talk about it later.' She wrenched her arm free, glared at him through the mist of tears she refused to shed. 'Because I'm not going.'

'What?' He stared at her as if she'd grown an extra head. 'Why not?'

How ironic, she thought as her hope shattered. That she should finally shock him out of his complacency, not with a declaration of love, but by the simple act of finally standing up for herself.

'Because I don't want to,' she said, her voice rising as she let the surge of temper take over to drown the pain. 'Because I told you I was falling in love with you and you don't even care enough about me to pretend it matters to you.' Her throat ached, her head hurt and her heart felt as if it were breaking into a thousand tiny pieces, but she made herself say what she should have said days ago. 'I didn't expect you to say it back. I'm not an idiot. We've only known each other ten days. But they've been the most wonderful ten days of my life... And I thought they meant something to you too.'

'This is ridiculous, Cassie,' Jace declared, mortified when his voice shook. 'You're overreacting.'

Unfortunately she wasn't the only one, he realised as panic clawed up his throat at the hopelessness on her face.

'Maybe from where you're standing,' she murmured, the brief magnificent show of temper dying as quickly as it had come. A tear dripped off her lashes, and sliced right through the charade of indifference he used to keep a tight rein on his temper. 'But from where I'm standing, I can see now I should have been honest with you much sooner.'

He grasped her arm again as she turned to leave. 'Damn it, Cassie. Can't you see how ridiculous you're being? What do you want me to say?' he said, sickened by the desperation in his voice. 'That I'm falling for you too? If you want me to say it I will.'

She faced him, the sadness in her gaze so much more painful than the anger. 'But you'd be lying, wouldn't you.' It wasn't a question. And how could he deny it when she was right? They were only words to him. A means to an end.

Maybe for a split second, when she'd said she was falling in love in that bright, excited tone, her body soft and pliant in his arms and her gaze glowing, he'd felt that strange sense of rightness, of completeness, but then the truth had registered. And he'd recoiled.

All he'd seen was his mother's face, her lip bleeding, her eyes blackened, her face bruised. And all the guilt and un-happiness, and the crushing feeling of hopelessness had risen up to strangle that ludicrous belief in the impossible.

Cassie grasped his wrist, pulled away from him. 'I can't come to New York.'

'Fine.' He fisted his fingers and buried them in his robe pockets, determined not to give in to the urge to touch her, to cling onto her, to force her to stay. He'd survive without her. Just as he'd survived before. 'I guess this is goodbye, then.'

He watched her lip tremble, but no more tears fell. Instead, she straightened, winning the fight for composure.

She disappeared into the bedroom, and he listened to the muted sounds as she got dressed and packed her bag while he clung onto the frigid control. So he could remain still and silent when she came out and said a quiet, 'Goodbye, Jace.'

But as the front door of the suite closed behind her he marched to the breakfast table, swept up the teacup she had been using and hurled it against the wall. Shattered china bounced on the thick carpet and tea dripped down the silk wallpaper as the old anger and resentment—and a sharp new pain—ripped through his chest.

CHAPTER SEVENTEEN

'HERE's fine, Dave,' Jace said tightly as the car slid into a space outside the imposing new glass-and-steel structure that housed Heathrow's Terminal Five.

'Are you sure you don't want me to park and help you with your bag, Mr Ryan?' the chauffeur asked through the partition.

'I've got it.' Stepping out of the car, he grasped his holdall. 'Thanks, Dave, you've done a great job.' Pulling five twenty-pound notes out of his wallet, he handed the tip through the window.

The driver smiled and handed Jace a business card. 'It's been a pleasure, Mr Ryan. Just give me a call next time you're in London.'

'Sure.' He gave the man a small salute as he drove off, then flicked the card into a nearby bin before walking into the terminal building.

He was never coming back to this godforsaken city again. Not if he could avoid it.

He'd taken a conference call with the buyers he'd chosen an hour ago and set the wheels in motion. Artisan would belong to someone else as soon as the markets opened tomorrow. He'd informed his PA to have his lawyer contact Helen's solicitors to organise the transfer of funds for her shares. And he'd still have a cool twenty-five mill to invest in his next venture.

He strode through the large, state-of-the-art terminal building, slinging the leather holdall carrying his essential stuff over his shoulder. He'd finally left all those lingering associations from his past behind once and for all. He had no ties to London, no ties to his ex-wife, and no ties to the young, driven and wildly ambitious man who had been so desperate to escape his childhood he'd done things that he'd later been ashamed of.

He was free at last. The last traces of his old life, his old self, were gone. He could start afresh.

The picture of Cassie, her small frame rigid as she walked away from him, flashed into his brain and made his steps falter.

He stopped, shut his eyes, banishing the image for about the five-hundredth time in the last three hours, and ignored the stuttering beat of his heart, and the piercing pain in his chest.

Pull yourself together, Ryan.

She'd done him a favour. He should never have invited her to New York in the first place. As soon as he got home, he'd be grateful that she wasn't going to be with him. And he'd done her a favour too. If he'd taken her to stay in his place in the East Village, knowing how she felt—or rather thought she felt—about him, it would have been even tougher to let her down gently when the time came for her to leave.

But even as he scanned the departure hall, spotted the first-class check-in for his flight to JFK and negotiated the snaking queues of suitcase-laden travellers to get to it, the stupid pain refused to go away. He could feel it like a jagged blade, stabbing at his composure again, slicing through his control just as it had done when the door had shut behind her.

Stop it. Stop thinking about her. She was never more than a good lay.

But even as he said the words in his head the pain and panic rose up his throat like bile and called him a liar.

Standing at the desk, he chucked his bag on the conveyor. 'Hi, my name's Jacob Ryan, I'm on flight three five three,' he said to the young check-in girl as he yanked his passport out of the inside pocket of his leather jacket, slapped it down on the desk. 'My PA, Jeannie Martin, was dealing with the ticket details.'

Just get on the damn plane. Once you're at fifty thousand feet the pain will be gone.

'Yes, Mr Ryan,' the check-in girl said perkily as she tapped his passport number into her computer, scanned it with easy efficiency.

But as hard as he tried to concentrate, on forgetting the memories, ignoring the pain, the sudden crippling sense of sadness, of loss and loneliness that he hadn't felt since he'd last seen his mother, forced its way past the boulder lodged in his throat, releasing a stream of images that flooded his subconscious in quick succession.

Cassie's wild hair and indignant pout as she'd hurled herself into his car; the determined frown as she tried to decide on the perfect gift for her best friend; the expectation on her face when she'd handed him the card she'd made—which was tucked in his jacket pocket because he'd been unable to throw it away while he packed; the soft weight of her lush little body curved against his side as they'd left the funfair; the sheen of tears, and the tenderness and understanding in her gaze when he'd told her about his stepfather; and the lilting hope in her voice when she'd announced she was falling in love.

If she'd only ever been a good lay, why wasn't it the thought of all the really amazing sex he was going to be missing that hurt the most now?

'I'm sorry, Mr Ryan. But we don't have your travelling companion's passport details. And the US Department of Homeland Security requires that—'

'What travelling companion?' he croaked, interrupting the stream of information.

'Ms Cassidy Fitzgerald,' she said, reading off the screen.

'But I...' Just the mention of her name out loud seemed to sharpen the pain unbearably. He swept his hand through his hair, feeling as if bits of him were being hacked off inside. 'How did you know?' he said dumbly. Was this some sort of weird alternative reality? Was he cracking up?

'How did I know what, Mr Ryan?'

'That she's meant to be travelling with me?'

The woman sent him a curious smile, then directed her gaze back to the screen. 'Ms Martin bought her ticket. Online at 1:30 a.m. last night London time. But we did email her to inform her that we would need...'

The woman's words trailed off as Jace recalled keying in the brief text message to Jeannie the night before, telling her to check availability on today's flight. And then the memory of the pleasure that had flooded his chest, that feeling of hope, of excitement, of rightness as he slung his mobile on the bedside table and watched Cassie step out of the bathroom. Her face soft and beautiful in the night light, her curves outlined through the wispy silk nightgown as she stood silhouetted in the doorway.

He'd taken her in the lobby as soon as they'd got back from the New Year's celebration. The passion so hot and raw it had consumed them both. But then she'd rushed off to the bathroom, and he'd waited for her, stretched out on the bed, anticipating how much he was going to enjoy taking her so slowly she begged, now the edge of their hunger had been satisfied.

He'd been so arrogant, so sure, that she was going to say yes to his offer, he'd passed the time by texting Jeannie to let her know he was planning to bring Cassie to New York. And with her usual efficiency his PA had done the rest.

But more than that, he hadn't for a moment worried about the implications of buying a ticket, because all he'd cared about in that instance was that Cassie would be with him, by his side, when he left.

He swore softly. The panic, the regret, the agony and desperation channelling into one simple conviction. He couldn't leave. Not without her. Not if he didn't want to go mad.

Gripping the handle of his holdall, his fingers no longer shaking, he picked the leather bag off the conveyer.

'Your boarding card, Mr Ryan.' The attendant handed the oblong strip of card over the counter.

'Keep it,' he said, his voice firm for the first time since Cassie had walked out. 'I don't need it now.'

CHAPTER EIGHTEEN

A TEARDROP splattered onto the drawing board, smudging the ink line, and Cassie stared at it in dismay. Grabbing a tissue from the box beside her easel, she swiped at her eyes, screwed the tissue up and launched it at the rubbish bin.

'Don't you dare cry,' she whispered to herself.

Placing shaking fingers to her lips, she took several deep breaths, trying to shrink the enormous boulder lodged in her throat. The little hiccup of emotion didn't bode well. She sniffed loudly.

What was wrong with her? It shouldn't hurt this much.

She was being unforgivably self-indulgent. Jace and she were never meant to be. All she'd done was fall into the same stupid, sentimental trap she'd fallen into before. Of believing a guy had stronger feelings for her than he actually had.

He'd made it perfectly clear that she'd blown their fling out of proportion and he didn't return her feelings.

She frowned, swallowing round the huge boulder. So why didn't she feel good about her decision? Why couldn't she stop wishing for the impossible?

Jace Ryan had said he didn't get involved. He'd told her that he didn't even do long-term relationships. She'd misinterpreted his invitation to New York. Put him on the spot and declared her feelings when she'd promised herself she wouldn't do that. But despite the fact that her timing sucked, it had still been the right thing to do to walk away. She didn't want to get her heart shattered just because she'd been foolish enough to believe he was falling for her too.

Cassie's bottom lip quivered. She bit into it, struggling to stem the maelstrom of emotion that had been pummelling her all day.

The only big glaring problem in her carefully worked out logic was that she wasn't falling in love with Jace. She'd fallen. Hard and fast and far too easily. And she was very much afraid that her foolish heart was already shattered.

She stared out of the bedroom's small window, the streetlight outside casting a yellow halo of light in the drizzle of freezing rain. Christmas was over. Jace would be on the plane now, flying back to his home in New York and out of her life.

She'd always regret what they had lost. Because however foolish she'd been, she hadn't been wrong to know she could have given him so much, that they could have given so much to each other.

But she'd offered him her heart and he hadn't wanted it. In the end she had to accept that and get over it. And however much it hurt now, she was much better moving on than struggling all on her own to make it work.

Today was the first day of a whole new year. She took in a deep breath, let it out slowly, glad to note it was only a little shaky. A whole new year and a whole new Cassie.

One day she'd find a guy who loved her the way she loved him. Who needed her and, more importantly, could give her what she needed. Lance had taken away her optimism and her self-respect and her belief in the power of love. And she had never even really loved him. Jace, for all his faults, and despite his resolute refusal to open himself to the possibility of love, had given her those gifts back. And for that she should be grateful.

Their wild Christmas fling hadn't been a mistake. It just hadn't been meant to last.

The loud thumping on the door made her jerk upright, and shattered the quiet moment of reflection.

Giving a little sigh, she climbed down from the stool and crossed to the front door. If that was Nessa, she'd allow herself a good solid cry on her shoulder, but she wouldn't let her best friend bad-mouth Jace. She didn't feel bitter, or used or angry, she just felt sad. But it was a sadness she knew she'd get over in time.

Sliding the deadbolt free, she wiped her eyes one last time and stiffened her stance. Time to give the new improved Cassie a workout. The Cassie who learned from her mistakes, but didn't let them change who she was as a person. But as she swung open the door she saw the handsome face that would likely haunt her dreams and the new improved Cassie turned tail and ran.

'Cass…'

She slammed the door in a flash of blind panic.

'Ow!' he yelled as the heavy oak hit the foot he'd wedged into the gap.

'Go away. You're supposed to be on a plane,' she shouted through the narrow opening.

She couldn't face him now, not after her pep talk. She had to begin the hard process of getting over him. This would only make it harder.

He wrapped his fingers round the door, shoved it back. 'Damn it. I think you've broken my foot.'

She stumbled back, bumped up against the sofa.

'That serves you right,' she said, stifling the prickle of guilt as he limped into the room. 'You shouldn't be here. I didn't invite you.'

'I don't care,' he said, looming over her, his eyes stormy

and his jaw rigid. 'I've come to get you. You're going to New York with me.'

'No, I'm not.' The anger that had been so unfamiliar that morning surged through her veins again, but this time she embraced it.

He had no right. No right to make her go through this all over again.

'Why not?' he said, exasperated, as he grasped her hips, dragged her towards him. 'You know you want to.'

She braced her hands against his chest. 'It's not that I don't want to. It's that I can't.'

'Why can't you? Because you told me you were falling for me?' He snapped the words, his own temper as volatile as hers. 'So what? We'll forget you ever said it. And everything can go back to the way it was before.'

She gasped, astonished not just by his gall, but by his ignorance. How could she be in love with a man who was so clueless about other people's feelings?

'I can't take it back.' She struggled out of his arms. 'That's the way I feel,' she said, her voice rising. 'And I can't stop feeling that way just because you don't.'

'Okay, fine.' He raked his hands through his hair, and she saw something that looked remarkably like panic. 'Feel that way if you want, but why should that stop us from continuing our affair? If you love me, why don't you want to be with me?' The puzzled anguish in his voice had her own temper cooling. How could he not know the answer to this? How could he understand so little about love?

'Because I'd want things you can't give me, Jace,' she said softly, willing him to understand. 'And that would destroy me in the end. Can't you see that?'

'How do you know I can't give you what you need?' he said, grasping her elbow, drawing her back into his arms.

'Maybe I could, if you gave me the chance. Why won't you let me try?'

As he pulled her close, wrapped his arms around her waist, she took a deep trembling breath of his scent and felt her resolve weakening.

'Please, Jace,' she whispered. 'Don't do this.'

She pressed her lips together to stop them trembling, pushed her forearms against his chest. She couldn't give in; she couldn't. Not when she'd come so far. If she went with him, knowing that he didn't love her, she'd only end up trying to convince herself again. She couldn't risk doing that. Not with him. Because with Jace it would be so much more devastating when she was finally forced to face the truth.

Then he touched his forehead to hers, placed a tender kiss on the tip of her nose and whispered, 'Please, Cassie, come with me. I can't go without you.'

The gulping sob racked her body, but she struggled against his grip and forced herself to step back. The tears flooded down her cheeks, the tears she'd held back all day, the tears she'd never shed over her father's neglect, or David's lack of interest or even Lance's betrayal. After thirteen short days, Jace had come to mean more to her than any of them. But as much as she wanted to reach out to him, she knew she couldn't.

'Don't cry, Cassie,' he said, reaching up to cradle her cheek. 'I didn't mean to make you cry. I don't want to hurt you.'

'I know you don't.' She shook her head, brushed the tears away as she crossed her arms under her breasts, lifted her chin to face him. 'But that isn't enough.'

'Then tell me what is?' he said.

She cocked her head to one side, finally acknowledging the desperation in his eyes, the unhappiness, the thin edge of control that was on the brink of shattering. And suddenly she understood how far he'd come. He did care about her, more than she suspected he had ever cared about any woman. He'd opened up to her in a way he probably never had before. The seed of hope that had refused to die pushed through her despair and confusion. Maybe this wasn't actually about her. Had she been unbelievably selfish and naive? Trying to force him to admit feelings that he didn't even understand?

'I need you to be honest about your feelings,' she said softly. 'Why can't you do that?'

He cursed under his breath. Then backed away, sat down heavily on the sofa. Sinking his head into his hands, he spoke, his voice muffled, but shaking with emotion. 'Because I don't want to love you. I don't want to love anyone.'

She sat beside him, placed her hand on his knee, the hope surging back to life now. At last she'd got behind the charm, the confidence and the cast-iron control, to the man beneath. 'Why not, Jace?'

'Because love is a mean, miserable, dirty little trick.' His voice cracked on the word. 'You think you can control it but you can't. And then it ends up controlling you.'

He sounded so angry, but behind the anger she could hear the fear.

'Why would you think that?' she asked gently, but she thought she already knew the answer. And her heart ached for him.

'Because that's exactly what happened to my mother.' He drew a sharp breath in, clasped his hands between his knees and stared blankly into the middle distance. 'She used to be so amazing. So sweet and kind and funny. When it was just the two of us.' His shoulder jerked in a tense shrug, but he didn't sound angry any more, just desperately sad. 'You know, before she met him.' He sucked in a shaky breath, blew it out slowly. 'When I was little and he hit me too, she'd say I should be more careful. That I knew he had a temper and I should try harder not to upset him.' The resigned sigh broke Cassie's heart. 'Then when I got older, and I was big enough to defend her, she hid the injuries. She'd say she walked into a door. Or she tripped and fell. She'd tell any stupid lie to protect him.' He ploughed his fingers through his hair. 'I tried to get her to report the abuse. And she wouldn't. Finally, I couldn't take any more. So I went to the police. She denied it all and kicked me out. That was the night before I got expelled.' He turned to face her. 'She never spoke to me again. All because she loved him.'

He looked shattered, exhausted, the dark memories swirling in his eyes. And her heart broke all over again for that traumatised child and the pitiable woman, destroyed by abuse, who had been unable to protect him.

Cassie covered his hand, threaded her fingers through his and held on, but refused to shed the tears that burned the backs of her eyes and blocked her throat. 'Jace, that wasn't love. Real love isn't a burden. It isn't a punishment. It doesn't hurt. Not intentionally. It heals.'

He stared at her, the muscles in his jaw tensing. 'How can you be sure?' he asked. And she knew in that moment she wasn't talking to the strong, confident, charismatic man, but to the angry and frightened child who had been taught to associate love with something twisted and ugly, a perverted mockery of the real thing.

'Because I love you, Jace. And I know that I would do everything in my power to stop you from being hurt.'

He closed his eyes, let his head drop back. As if absorbing the words. Then he huffed out a strained laugh and slanted her a sideways look. 'Apart from breaking my foot, you mean.'

Her lips tilted, joy surging through her. 'That was an accident. You shouldn't have stuck your foot in the doorway.'

She stroked her hands down his cheeks, then placed her

lips on his, putting all the love and longing she felt into the slow, tender kiss.

His hands grasped her head and he thrust his tongue inside her mouth, deepening the kiss. She opened for him, her tongue tangling with his, tasting his need and desperation as the hot rush of desire eddied up from her core. And the love bloomed inside her, like a garden leaving winter behind and welcoming spring.

This was right. He was right. She hadn't imagined his feelings. They had been as strong as her own. He just hadn't been able to articulate them, because of a childhood marred by violence that had left him terrified to admit them. To even identify them.

He lifted his head, his cheeks flushed, his eyes dark with much more than desire. 'I couldn't get on that plane and leave you behind, even though I tried to make myself.' His eyes roamed over her face. 'When I'm with you, you make me feel that I'm a better person than I'll ever be without you.' His eyes met hers at last and she could see the depth of emotion reflected in them. 'I don't want to tell you I love you, because in the end they're just words to me. Words that I've never trusted. But I can tell you I want to be with you. I want to try and make this work. Whatever *this* is,' he said, sounding unsure of himself, and desperately vulnerable. 'Is that enough for you?'

Tears welling in her eyes, she gave a delighted chuckle. 'That's more than enough.'

As he hugged her close, buried his head in her hair and murmured, 'Thank God for that,' she wondered if he had any idea that he'd just told her he loved her in every way that mattered.

EPILOGUE

'THIS is the absolute last stop,' Jace murmured into his wife's hair, breathing in the cinnamon scent as they stood on the pavement, admiring Selfridges' Christmas window display. 'You've got exactly ten minutes to enjoy the view and then I'm hauling you back to the hotel,' he said firmly, determined not to get sidetracked again. 'No arguments, Mrs Ryan.' He spanned his hands across the firm mound of her belly and drew her back against his chest, his heart jolting into his throat—as it always did when he thought of the child growing inside her. 'I don't care how many presents you've still got to buy.'

They'd been Christmas shopping for three solid hours by his count, and he wanted her back at The Chesterton with her feet up for the rest of the day, before they headed to Nessa and Terrence's place tomorrow for the annual Christmas Day get-together. After the six-hour flight from New York the day before, he was still struggling with jet lag so she must be too. And she was seven months pregnant for heaven's sake. She had to be exhausted.

Cassie laughed and leaned into him. Her palms covered the backs of his hands. 'Don't be such a spoilsport. I'm absolutely fine. And so is Junior.' She tilted her head. 'Now, what do you think of that little red fire engine?' she asked, pointing at the display of traditional children's toys expertly arranged around a silver Christmas tree.

'Oh, no, you don't!' Pulling her round to face him, he slipped his hands beneath her heavy wool coat and held her against him, the round swell of her belly butting his stomach. 'We're not going back in there. The baby's not due 'til February. It can do without a Christmas present.' He kissed her forehead, trying to keep a grip on his frustration. The woman was addicted to Christmas shopping and he wasn't going to feed her damn addiction a moment longer. 'And anyway, the doctor wasn't one hundred per cent sure that was a penis on the scan. It might be a girl.'

'Who says girls can't like fire engines?' she announced. 'You never know, if we have a daughter she might want to be a firefighter.' Flattening her hands against the emerald cashmere she'd bought him three Christmases ago, she grinned up at him. His heart did the little flip-flop it always did when he looked into her expressive face and saw the love she never disguised. 'But that'll have to be next time,' she purred, her eyes twinkling with mischief. 'Because believe me, that was definitely a penis.'

He huffed out a strained laugh, his throat thickening at the memory of that grainy three-dimensional image. But the mention of a 'next time' had the twin tides of terror and excitement surging past his larynx and threatening to cut off his air supply.

Just as they'd been doing consistently for the last seven months. Ever since she'd sat in his lap in their loft apartment in the East Village one morning, wrapped her arms round his shoulders with a calm and decidedly smug smile on her face and announced they were having a baby.

It shouldn't have been that much of a shock. They'd been discussing parenthood for months and—after Cassie had managed to talk him off the ledge of abject panic her original suggestion had caused and finally convinced him that there wasn't a damn thing stopping him from being a decent father—they had agreed to stop using contraception two weeks before. But even so, no way was he contemplating doing this again until Junior was safely out and about—and quite possibly choosing college courses.

'There's not going to be next time,' he said. 'Not until my blood pressure is back to normal. And certainly not until you learn to behave appropriately when you're seven months pregnant.'

A tiny frown creased her brow. 'But I just have to—'

'No, you don't,' he interrupted.

'Only one more…' She shifted, trying to make a break for it, but he held on, keeping her firmly plastered against him.

'We can come back after Christmas for the sales,' he said, although he'd be reserving judgement on that if she didn't get enough sleep in the next few days. 'But there'll be no more shopping today. I can see how exhausted you are.'

Her lips formed into a mutinous pout, so he dipped his head, touched his forehead to hers and brought out the big guns. 'I love you to bits, Mrs Cassidy Ryan. And I love this baby—with or without a penis. And there's no way I'm risking the only two things I care about in this world because you are a shopaholic.'

She melted against him, as he knew she would, and let out a heavy sigh. 'That's not playing fair.' Her hands lifted to caress the side of his head, her fingers threading into his hair as his hands settled on her waist. 'You know I can't resist when you say things like that.'

He chuckled. 'Tough.'

To think he'd once found it so hard to say the words to her.

He was so far removed from that man now—he could barely remember him. The man who'd hidden his resentment and his loneliness and his inadequacy behind a veneer of arrogance and lazy charm, and had been so terrified of commitment he'd refused to nurture the simplest of relationships. Cassie had come into his life and changed everything. In the space of three years all the fear and anger and guilt of his childhood had faded to be replaced by a happiness, a contentment, a companionship he had never even believed existed. She was his soul mate, his kindred spirit and every wet dream he'd ever had—all rolled into one.

Because he knew how lucky he was to have found her. He told Cassie he loved her whenever he felt like it now. Which was so damn often, he was in danger of becoming a Hallmark card. But he didn't care. Because it was the truth. And if telling her made her putty in his hands—well, that was just a nice fringe benefit, which he was more than prepared to use whenever the need arose.

Slinging an arm over her shoulder, he directed her away from Selfridges' imposing art deco facade and hailed a cab, secure in the knowledge that he'd won. For now.

'Come on.' He hugged her, kissed the top of her hair. 'This store has been here close to a century. It'll still be here on Boxing Day. I promise.'

Cassie snuggled under Jace's arm as he shouted out their destination to the taxi driver and let his warmth wrap around her. She flexed her feet in her boots, her arches screaming in agony, rubbed her hand over her belly where the baby had finally stopped punching her and felt exhaustion wash over her.

'You're having a nap when we get back to the suite,' Jace declared in that dictatorial tone that he'd been using rather too often recently, as he settled back into the seat and drew her into his arms.

She glanced up to encounter his stern no-nonsense look— and took a deep breath. The clean scent of his soap invaded her senses as his heartbeat hammered under her palm. The familiar flutter of desire pulsed deep in her sex, as love made her heart fly off into the cosmos. She cocked an eyebrow at him, then let her palm drift down the worn, whisper-soft cashmere and felt his abdominal muscles tense beneath.

Gotcha.

'I'm only having a nap if you have one with me,' she murmured. He might have sucker punched her with that declaration of love—something he'd become remarkably adept at doing, she'd noticed—but she wasn't a complete pushover. And she knew just how to sucker punch him right back.

He gave a soft half-laugh. 'No way. You're sleeping this afternoon.' He brushed his thumb across her cheekbone. 'No hanky-panky until those shadows under your eyes have gone.'

'Jace,' she said, letting her fingers delve under the cashmere to encounter the lightly furred skin of his flat belly. 'You really don't want to deny a pregnant lady when she's tired and horny—or she may get cranky.'

Swearing softly, he grasped her hand, halting its descent under his belt, but she'd already seen the flash of desire in his eyes, and the muscle tense in his jaw, which signalled his arousal. And she knew she had him.

She grinned. 'And mind-blowing orgasms always help me sleep more soundly, so it's your duty to supply one.'

'You little...' he muttered, gripping her fingers and bringing them to his mouth. He kissed the knuckles, his gaze alight with laughter and dark with lust. 'All right, damn it. Have it your way. We'll take the nap together.'

'With full hanky-panky privileges,' she clarified. The swell of love and contentment squeezed her heart as arousal stampeded through her system.

She adored this man so much. His honesty, his integrity, his sense of humour, his surly, sexy magnetism and that protective instinct that made her feel so safe and so secure. But most of all she adored the fact that she could love him without having to hold any piece of herself back, because she knew she could trust him to do the same.

She could still remember the first time he'd actually told her he loved her. And she'd made a huge fuss, because she could see how big a deal it had been for him—being able to trust his feelings enough to say the words. But the truth was, she had never needed to hear him say them—even though they had the power to melt her into an emotional puddle every time he'd said them since—because it was the love those three simple words represented that mattered. And he'd already shown her, in so many ways, that she already had that.

'You can have full hanky-panky privileges,' he agreed as his hand settled on her thigh, making the silk of her dress slide over sensitised skin. 'Within reason.' He slanted his lips across hers, gave her a deep, seeking kiss that promised at least one mind-blowing orgasm before naptime.

He smiled down at her as he pulled away. 'Consider it an early Christmas present, Mrs Ryan. But be warned, I plan to seduce you into a coma—and once I'm done with you, you're going to want to sleep for a week.'

She giggled at the seductive boast. 'And miss Christmas tomorrow? I don't think so. But you have my permission to give it your best shot.'

'Don't worry, I intend to.'

As the cab pulled up at the entrance to The Chesterton, the sparkle of Christmas lights in the winter greenery reminded her of the first time she'd arrived at the luxury hotel, in a wet coat and muddy boots, with Nessa's saucy suggestion that she find herself a candy man turning her head.

Paying the driver and stepping out of the cab, the man who had become so much more to her than that hauled out her many bags of shopping and passed them to the waiting doorman with instructions to have them sent to their suite.

As Jace ducked back into the cab to offer her his hand her

heart fluttered at the devastating smile on his face. 'Come on, lover, your candy coma awaits,' he joked, as if he had read her thoughts.

She laughed as she placed her fingers on his rough palm and let him lead her out of the cab. But as she walked up the steps, his arm secure around her waist, emotion welled up in her throat. The thrill of the night ahead, the thought of the Christmas celebrations to come tomorrow, the wonder of the new life growing inside her and the exciting promise of what her future held with Jace by her side soon had the emotion overwhelming her, and making the fairy lights blur.

'Hey, now.' He stopped on the top step, pushed her chin up to examine her face. 'What's with the waterworks?' he asked, concern shadowing his eyes. 'No crying allowed. It's Christmas tomorrow. That's your favourite day of the year.'

'They're happy tears, you twit.' She nudged him with her elbow. 'And FYI, Christmas isn't my favourite day any more,' she said, sniffing back the silly tears that had become a constant companion ever since she'd become pregnant. 'Now I have you, every day is.'

His slow, sexy smile made her heart race into her throat, and the moisture spill over her lids. 'Well, that's good news,' he murmured, reaching into his pocket for a tissue. 'Because when I win the candy war tonight, and seduce you into that coma,' he said, gently dabbing at her cheeks to stem the flow, 'you're going to miss Christmas tomorrow.'

She didn't miss Christmas. Not quite. But it was an extremely close call.

* * * * *

CLASSIC

Quintessential, modern love stories
that are romance at its finest.

EXTRA

COMING NEXT MONTH from Harlequin Presents®
AVAILABLE DECEMBER 27, 2011

**#3035 PASSION AND
THE PRINCE**
Penny Jordan

**#3036 THE GIRL THAT
LOVE FORGOT**
The Notorious Wolfes
Jennie Lucas

**#3037 SURRENDER TO
THE PAST**
Carole Mortimer

**#3038 HIS POOR LITTLE
RICH GIRL**
Melanie Milburne

**#3039 IN BED WITH
A STRANGER**
The Fitzroy Legacy
India Grey

**#3040 SECRETS OF
THE OASIS**
Abby Green

COMING NEXT MONTH from Harlequin Presents® EXTRA
AVAILABLE JANUARY 10, 2012

**#181 IN A STORM OF
SCANDAL**
Irresistible Italians
Kim Lawrence

**#182 A DANGEROUS
INFATUATION**
Irresistible Italians
Chantelle Shaw

**#183 WORKING WITH THE
ENEMY**
Risky Business
Susan Stephens

**#184 THERE'S SOMETHING
ABOUT A REBEL...**
Risky Business
Anne Oliver

You can find more information on upcoming Harlequin® titles,
free excerpts and more at www.HarlequinInsideRomance.com.

HPECNM1211

REQUEST YOUR
FREE BOOKS!

2 FREE NOVELS PLUS
2 FREE GIFTS!

USA TODAY bestselling author

Penny Jordan

brings you her newest romance

PASSION
AND THE PRINCE

Prince Marco di Lucchesi can't hide his proud
disdain for fiery English rose Lily Wrightington—
or his attraction to her! While touring the palazzos
of northern Italy, the atmosphere heats up…until
shadows from Lily's past come out….

*Can Marco keep his passion under wraps
enough to protect her, or will it unleash itself, too?*

Find out in January 2012!

*Brittany Grayson survived a horrible ordeal at the hands
of a serial killer known as The Professional…
who's after her now?*

*Harlequin® Romantic Suspense presents a new installment
in Carla Cassidy's reader-favorite miniseries,*
LAWMEN OF BLACK ROCK.

Enjoy a sneak peek of
TOOL BELT DEFENDER.

*Available January 2012
from Harlequin® Romantic Suspense.*

"**B**rittany?" His voice was deep and pleasant and made
her realize she'd been staring at him openmouthed through
the screen door.

"Yes, I'm Brittany and you must be…" Her mind suddenly went blank.

"Alex. Alex Crawford, Chad's friend. You called him
about a deck?"

As she unlocked the screen, she realized she wasn't
quite ready yet to allow a stranger inside, especially a male
stranger.

"Yes, I did. It's nice to meet you, Alex. Let's walk around
back and I'll show you what I have in mind," she said. She
frowned as she realized there was no car in her driveway.
"Did you walk here?" she asked.

His eyes were a warm blue that stood out against his
tanned face and was complemented by his slightly shaggy
dark hair. "I live three doors up." He pointed up the street to
the Walker home that had been on the market for a while.

"How long have you lived there?"

"I moved in about six weeks ago," he replied as they

walked around the side of the house.

That explained why she didn't know the Walkers had moved out and Mr. Hard Body had moved in. Six weeks ago she'd still been living at her brother Benjamin's house trying to heal from the trauma she'd lived through.

As they reached the backyard she motioned toward the broken brick patio just outside the back door. "What I'd like is a wooden deck big enough to hold a barbecue pit and an umbrella table and, of course, lots of people."

He nodded and pulled a tape measure from his tool belt. "An outdoor entertainment area," he said.

"Exactly," she replied and watched as he began to walk the site. The last thing Brittany had wanted to think about over the past eight months of her life was men. But looking at Alex Crawford definitely gave her a slight flutter of pure feminine pleasure.

Will Brittany be able to heal in the arms of Alex,
her hotter-than-sin handyman…or will a second
psychopath silence her forever? Find out in
TOOL BELT DEFENDER
Available January 2012
from Harlequin® Romantic Suspense
wherever books are sold.

ALWAYS POWERFUL, PASSIONATE AND PROVOCATIVE.

USA TODAY BESTSELLING AUTHOR

KATHIE DeNOSKY

BRINGS YOU ANOTHER STORY FROM

TEXAS CATTLEMAN'S CLUB: THE SHOWDOWN

Childhood rivals Brad Price and Abigail Langley have found themselves once again in competition, this time for President of the Texas Cattleman's Club. But when Brad's plans are interrupted when his baby niece is suddenly placed under his care, he finds himself asking Abigail for help. As Election Day draws near, will Brad still be going after the Presidency or Abigail's heart? Find out in:

IN BED WITH THE OPPOSITION

Available December wherever books are sold.